Return to Me

Return to Me

A Tycoon's Temptation Romance

Michele Arris

TULE
PUBLISHING

Author's Note

Though inspired by actual places, please note that some events and locations mentioned in this book are fictional and are meant solely for you to escape and enjoy.

Acknowledgements

Once again, I got the tremendous pleasure to work with the amazing Julie Sturgeon. Julie, I'm so fortunate to continue to have you by my side throughout this series. I cannot express enough how much I appreciate the amazing way you assist me in developing my stories.

Leena Hyat, thank you for all the effort you put in to getting my cover just right.

Thank you to Jane Porter, Meghan Farrell, Nikki Babri and the entire Tule Publishing team for being a terrific group to work with, and for the continued dedication you give to each and every story.

A very special thank you to my dear friend, Delena Pratt. Before the first draft was even on paper, you were there helping me mold the hero and heroine. I remember one time in particular where we spent hours fleshing out Vincent and Evie's world. You were a big part of that.

My heartfelt thank you to my family for their constant cheers.

Finally, dear readers, I'm immensely grateful for your continued support. I'm eager to share more amazing stories with you.

Chapter One

EVIE SAT ON the bench at her vanity and slathered her body in fragrant moisturizer before applying her makeup. She couldn't recall the last time she'd worn a full face. As a pastry chef, staring into a hot oven, and hands deep in moist dough most of the day, there simply wasn't a need for it.

She hastily picked up the damp bath towel from the floor and rushed to neatly fold it, feeling that familiar twinge tightening her skin. But she caught herself. Some habits, even forced ones—Patrick expected tidiness—were hard to break. She tossed the weighted Turkish cotton blend onto the counter and went to her adjoining closet.

Beneath bright recessed lighting, designer dresses hung from heavy brushed nickel rods. Shoes and handbags lined pristine white shelves. The large, thick slab of gray travertine set atop a center island that housed drawers filled with high-quality silk and satin undergarments.

Just about every extravagance in her wardrobe had been purchased by her husband. Patrick called them gifts. But she saw them for what they were: his way to control her all the way down to her bare flesh.

Ann, as my wife, you must present yourself appropriately.

He never called her Evie, preferring her middle name. He'd expressed it was a loving sentiment shared only between them, so she'd allowed it. But later toward the end of the marriage during one of his many outbursts, he'd said *Evie* sounded *infantile*.

She was required to dress to the nines. Fine crystal had to sparkle, and silverware had to be properly set at every meal.

Evie looked around the spacious room that was about the size of some of D.C.'s studio apartments. *Seven years. How did I endure it for so long?*

With a good mental shake, which seemed to be happening more and more lately, it brought her back to the matter at hand.

Well, the Vera Wang blush-pink sheath dress looked professional enough. Its three-quarter-length, color-matched trench coat should provide adequate comfort for the DMV's forecasted high-sixty-degrees, early summer afternoon.

She slipped her feet into a pair of high-arched, dove-gray leather pumps and grabbed the matching handbag that had been used once or twice at most.

With her red wire-framed glasses in place, she pinned the top of her hair away from her face, letting the rest drape loosely at her shoulders. Her dark toffee curls tended to frizz if someone so much as exhaled too heavily.

After a quick look in the full-length mirror, she headed down the ornate curved stairs into the foyer, her heels clipping along the smooth marble. With each step, the echo that resonated beneath her feet and bounced off the bare walls was a constant reminder of Patrick pilfering the expensive artwork on his departure.

Dixie and Percy made their delightful presence known with the rattle of their cage over in the living room. Evie made a quick trip to the kitchen and grabbed a large handful of baby carrots, then brought the furry pair their veggie breakfast. She'd been caring for her friend and business partner Tabitha's dwarf rabbits. On strict bedrest with a high-risk pregnancy, Tab had been instructed not to lift a finger.

The security monitor chimed—the only accoutrement adorning the otherwise naked, beige walls. A young Uber driver stared into the viewer at the privacy gate. She tapped the display, releasing the lock, and the heavy iron gates slowly parted. She hurried out the front door as the driver came into the circular driveway and stopped just shy of the flagstone steps. The car's interior had a surprisingly pleasant pine scent. Her last ride carried a pungent aroma of pizza with a hefty sprinkle of gym sweat.

"Afternoon, ma'am." The young man smiled, wide and white, his blond ponytail secured in a topknot, the sides and back of his head shaven smooth. The Georgetown University tassel dangled from the volume dial as he lowered Ed Sheeran's "Beautiful People" to an almost rhythmic hum.

Does being thirty-one merit the title "ma'am"?

"Good afternoon."

"The temp's dropped since this morning. Let me know if you need me to add some heat. I grew up in Southern California…anything below seventy is cold to me." He chuckled.

"I'm sure." She returned a smile to the one beaming back at her in the rearview mirror.

"Nice house," he said as they rolled away and cleared the gates that closed on the five-and-a-half-acre estate.

Evie looked back at the finely crafted double doors that cleverly sealed in her secrets. Three-car garage with boat storage capacity, eight bedrooms, ten bathrooms, home theater, pool house—just shy over fourteen thousand square feet of living space. The contradiction was never lost on her: so much space when she was perpetually restrained. She situated herself in the back seat of the tan Ford Focus. Her BMW was in Patrick's name. He'd sought to punish her by taking the vehicle on his exit as well. *Asshole.*

They rode along in respectable silence until her cell phone ringing cut into the long stretch of relaxing quiet. She checked the display and opened the line.

"Hi, Mom."

"Hello, my darling. You didn't return my call last night. I was getting concerned."

Her mom was clingy, but Evie didn't mind. They chatted or sent one another a quick text practically every day. "Sorry, I was exhausted. I had to do inventory and didn't leave the bakery until after ten last night."

"Sweetheart, you're the boss. That's something your staff can handle. Learn to delegate. Now, what is this I hear about you firing your attorney? Kate was over for lunch yesterday. She told your father and me you terminated Gerald Sigler's services. Does this mean you've decided to reconcile with Patrick?"

It was no surprise Mr. Sigler told her soon-to-be ex-mother-in-law, Kate, who in turn told Evie's parents he'd been dismissed. She recently discovered Sigler was acquainted with her ex's family, which was one of the reasons he was no longer her attorney.

"Patrick and I haven't reconciled. I'm hiring another lawyer. As a matter of fact, I'm on my way to my first meeting with him now."

"Maybe you can take this moment to reconsider your decision to end your marriage. Or at least seek the advice of a marriage counselor as Mr. Sigler suggested. It wouldn't hurt to try."

Evie rolled her eyes skyward. She needed to reconcile with who she was, what she deserved, and what she wanted in her future—the six months it took to decide to file for divorce after leaving her husband had been in itself counseling.

"Mom, I've been separated from Patrick for a year now and filed divorce papers with Mr. Sigler about six months ago, but I'm still waiting for an arbitration date. He's simply far too busy with more important clients. And I'm certain it's the only reason he suggested counseling. It would buy him time."

"Charlotte, if she wants to hire her own attorney, it's her choice."

Apparently, her mom had her on speakerphone. "Hi, Dad."

"How's my buttercup?"

Henry Langston had given Evie that nickname the first day she crossed their threshold at four years old. The Langstons officially adopted her at age nine. A little black girl taken in by a white suburban couple, she'd found offense at being called something that was one stem shy of a weed.

When asked why he called her buttercup, he simply said, "Like the flower, your smile is beautiful and abundant." And she'd been his shining sun ever since.

"Dad, I'm fine. Just running a little behind for my appointment."

"Are you enjoying your new bakery space? I had a good time at the grand opening. The food was delicious. What were those little doughy things with chocolate in the center? I think I ate about a hundred of them."

Evie smiled. There were several *doughy things with chocolate in the center.* "Maybe a truffle."

"It's just…you ended your marriage so abruptly," her mom cut in, evidently intent on continuing her point. "Kate said her son felt blindsided by the separation. Frankly, so were your father and I."

"Charlotte, let's not—" her dad started.

Evie drew back against the seat. "Blindsided! Patrick told you and his mother he was blindsided?"

You're supposed to be a chef. I have yet to get a decent steak. In his disapproval, the sirloin along with the plate was tossed into the trash while Evie was told what a mediocre cook she was. Newly folded laundry was often dumped on the floor because he decided she'd done a piss-poor job of it. Throw pillows had to be fluffed and perfectly creased in the center. Dusting and polishing the furniture had to happen, at minimum, twice a week or the house was considered a pigsty. And all while she worked a fifteen-hour day at the bakery. Everything in its place—a significant, cognitive characteristic underlying obsessive-compulsive personality disorder. With one of her three degrees being in psychology and having read hours of case studies on the topic, Evie was always sensitive to his condition. Hiring a housekeeper was out of the question. Patrick's OCPD tended to rule him. But he also used it as a way to control.

Countless moments he berated and degraded her self-worth. And he wouldn't stop until the sheen of tears glistened in her eyes. Then he'd cover his torment and hurt with a new diamond pendant necklace or a designer dress and heels, or even a fashionable handbag, while blaming his abhorrent behavior on the stresses of working under the thumb of her father. Her teeth would ache from the syrupy sweetness of his kindness that followed his cruelty.

Patrick was smart and cunning and knew how to abuse her without leaving a mark. Her scars were mental. But she wasn't a failure simply because her marriage had failed, and she'd found the strength to walk away. Yet she kept those bruises hidden from her family. Failure was unacceptable in the Langston household. If something broke, you got a wrench and fixed it.

"Mom, Patrick's not the saint you take him for."

"I never said he was. He has admitted to us that he's made mistakes, but he's been working on himself. Numerous times he has said to Kate and me how much he wants to reconcile. Evie, dear—" her voice softened into that warm, motherly timbre "—he loves you."

And that was why Evie didn't talk about it. Patrick had an ally in her mom. The fact that her mother-in-law and her mom had become good friends didn't help.

"I don't—" Evie paused when the driver shot a glance at her over his shoulder.

"Something's happening over there." He pointed at the stopped ambulance holding up traffic, its lights whirling a few steps from the building where she was headed. Cars began merging from two lanes into one, forced by a police cruiser parked at an angle in the middle of the street.

"Mom, Dad, I have to go. I'll call later."

"Love you," both said together.

"Love you, too." She looked at her watch—2:34. "I'll walk the rest of the way." With her purse secured at the crook of her arm, she scooted to the opposite seat, closest to the curb, and got out. "Thank you."

A brisk strut brought her to the building where law firm—Slate, Ellis, Wardell, and Scott, LLP—took up the entire eleventh and twelfth floors.

Scott. Vincent Scott. Her stomach lurched. Before entering, she fished in her handbag for her mirror and freshened her lip gloss. Hair still looked decent enough. She smoothed a hand down her dress. He once said pink brought out the golden glow in her fair brown skin.

Shit. What the hell am I doing? One would think after twelve years she'd have no reaction to the mere brush of his name. In fact, there should be a deep-seated loathing that churned and soured in her gut for the man who walked out of her life without a word those many years ago. Yet here she was making certain her appearance was on point in case she ran into Vincent Scott. It being his law practice, the likelihood was high.

She never would've imagined Vincent becoming an attorney. And from what she'd heard, he kicked ass at it. His firm handled high-profile sorts who expected a certain level of discretion. She required that type of firepower to deal with Patrick's legal camp. Those bully bulldogs were intent on stripping her of everything. So, yes, she needed an attorney just as ruthless. Thankfully, it didn't mean she had to work with Scott. There was a long list of other lawyers at the firm, like the one she was about to meet. That said, enduring Scott's dismissive coldness was all but unavoidable, since her best friend, Kennedi Chase, was about to marry Vincent's best friend, Trenton Shaw. *Small damn world.* Some things were simply out of her control.

The woman seated behind the security desk, the closest of the two guards on duty, came to her feet the moment Evie cleared the revolving glass door.

"Good afternoon. I'm Evie Powell here to see Leonard Rosati."

"Just a minute."

As the guard spoke on the phone, Evie, along with the other security personnel, watched through the glass entrance the police officer directing traffic. "I wonder what happened. Did someone get—?"

"Mrs. Powell?"

She turned to the woman.

"Go to eleven and see Jasmine at the receptionist desk."

"Thanks." She took the elevator up. The doors split open to a whirl of commotion. *Oh—!* She leaped out of the way as two EMTs came barreling toward her with a man seated partially upright upon a gurney, eyes shut, oxygen mask affixed to his sweaty face, and a blood pressure monitor strapped to his arm.

"Mrs. Powell?"

She twirled and met a tall, African American woman. "Yes?"

"I'm Jasmine. It's—Excuse me." The young woman turned away and gave a tap at the headset positioned at her ear. After offering what sounded like directions to their location, she turned back. "Can I take your jacket?"

"Thanks." Evie shuffled out of the trench while catching last sight of the poor soul struggling to breath as the elevator doors sealed him within. "Is this a bad time?"

Jasmine dashed to the closet at the right of the receptionist's desk, then returned. "You were to see Mr. Rosati—I'm sorry. One moment." She tapped her headset once more.

The atmosphere hummed, conversations intersecting. People went about their business—Jasmine included—as if they hadn't just witnessed a man getting carted off on a stretcher, as though it was merely another day at the office.

Jasmine ended her call. "Sorry about that. My counterpart on twelve is out sick today. His calls are rerouted to me. Now, as I was about to say, I'm afraid Mr. Rosati has taken ill. That was him you saw with the EMTs."

Evie's eyes bulged. "Oh goodness!"

"We'll get an update soon on his condition, I'm sure. In the meantime, alternative arrangements have been made. Please follow me."

"I can postpone. Clearly, this isn't a good time."

"I assure you the firm has everything under control." She extended a hand toward the stairs and started off.

Evie kept in close step as they moved through the bustling activity of power-suited professionals and took a set of glossy pine stairs up to the next floor.

It was a luxurious suite of spotless glass, high-polished finishes, and rich ivory leather furnishings. The décor said the retainer fee would bite deep into her wallet. If her attorney did his job right, Patrick would be footing the bill. On that note—

"Is Mr. Rosati all right?"

Jasmine glanced back while never missing a strut. "His assistant will provide an update when it becomes available. With his absence, the senior partners understand the concern you have as well as the rest of Mr. Rosati's clients when news of his abrupt departure is made known. But no worries. They've decided to divide his roster among them." There was an excited lift in her otherwise monotone voice. "In other words, you'll get to work with one of the four top legal counsels here. You can't go wrong; they're all amazing."

That familiar knot coiled in Evie's belly. She touched Jasmine's arm, slowing her determined stride. "Senior partners? Which senior partner?"

"I'm not sure. Everything happened so fast. The four are meeting as we speak to decide who gets which case." Jasmine continued forward.

The twelfth floor was even more posh than the one below. Wall upon wall of glass separated spacious executive office suites. They entered a rather large conference room.

"Hope you don't mind; this is the only meeting space unoccupied. It's been a crazy day. Please have a seat. Can I get you some coffee? Tea?" She gestured to three Keurigs and a host of condiments that lined the credenza on the other side of the room.

"No, thank you."

"Good afternoon, Mrs. Powell."

They turned, and Evie's stomach did yet another roller coaster-quick drop as she stared back into the very eyes she didn't wish to see. Why did her damn luck always have to misfire? "Afternoon, Mr. Scott."

They'd done well at maintaining their distance when around their mutual friends: Kennedi and Trenton. She'd prefer to keep it that way.

Jasmine looked between them. "You've already met?"

"Yes," both Evie and Vincent said in unison, dryly.

Aside from the tightness Evie saw in his strong, angular jaw, there was hardly a hint of readable expression in his otherwise handsome, smooth-shaven, honeycomb-brown features. No surprise. Whenever they were forced to tolerate sharing the same space, it was as if he looked right through her, as if she didn't exist. His blatant disregard annoyed her more than any cruel words would. It was he who'd ended their relationship practically a lifetime ago when he chose to disappear out of her life without a word.

"Thank you for handling the situation with Leonard. I heard you acted swiftly. The partners and I appreciate it."

"I've notified Mr. Rosati's wife," Jasmine said. "She'll call with an update on his condition. Oh, and I ordered flowers."

"Appreciate it. What would I do without you?"

"Let me know if you need anything." A wide, gift-giving grin spread across Jasmine's face as she soaked up her boss's praise. "Excuse me, I have a call coming in." With a tap at her ear, she closed the door on her way out.

So that's how it is? Evie observed that his deadpan expression had filled with warmth as he addressed his receptionist, contrary to the iceberg chill he tended to project toward her.

Her heels sank into the ultra-thick carpet pile. Luxurious, rich maplewood walls; crystal pendant lighting; top-grade audiovisual; three enormous, mounted flat screens; and a direct backdrop view of the Washington Monument in the distance—Vincent had done well for himself. A far cry from what his life goals had been when they'd dated.

"I have to say, I was surprised to learn you became a lawyer. You once said the profession robs one of his soul." She chuckled lightly, and he didn't crack even a hint of a grin.

"Situations in life provoke change. And I'm damn good at what I do here, if that's what you're really asking." He regarded her as he released the two buttons on his dark suit that fitted to the seams.

Okay. Ice effectively unbroken.

A perfectly Windsor-knotted silk tie and polished, black wing-tip shoes. Quite the contrast to the well-worn Jimmy Hendrix T-shirt, motor-oil-stained jeans, and Timberlands she remembered.

She'd hardly recognized him several months ago when he showed up at the bakery, looking for her friend and business partner, Kennedi. The contempt that had flooded his features when he'd spotted Evie that day was unmistakable. The feeling had been mutual, and not much had changed since their surprise reunion. To that end, today she'd try to be civil.

"What I meant was, you were pretty determined to open an autobody repair shop." She rested her hands atop the spine of one of the twenty or so buttery-soft, high-back leather chairs, needing something to fill her palms to alleviate the tension. "I recall how much you loved working on cars. All you could talk about was owning a garage."

"Who said I didn't? And you were pretty determined to marry well." The subtle curve of the corner of his lips was clearly mocking as he opened his portfolio and started scanning the pages. "We should get started." His gaze moved over her, resting on significant points of her frame, then returned to his notes. Admiration or abhorrence? His stoic demeanor gave no clue either way. "There's coffee." Without looking up, he gestured over at the credenza and pulled out his chair but didn't sit when Evie chose to remain standing.

Civility simply wasn't going to happen between them. "Look, no need for us to torture ourselves. It was Kennedi's suggestion that I consider soliciting your firm. Given our history, I had reservations about it, but after speaking with Mr. Rosati, I thought I'd give it a try. Lord knows I need a good divorce attorney. You have three other partners, not to mention thirty or so junior level, like that of Leonard Rosati's capabilities. Please hand my case over to one of them."

His eyes met hers. Flat. Steady. "There are other counsels within the firm who could take your case. But as a courtesy to Leonard, my partners and I are handling his client list. We each have our specialty. If you want the best, I'm the most practiced in dealing with high-profile and messy divorces. From what I gathered of Rosati's notes so far, your situation falls into the latter category. If you think our past involvement will have any impact on how I'll litigate, I can assure you it won't." He resumed scanning the pages, then looked up again, a slow glide of his gaze from her head to her heels.

A blatant scrutiny. "From where I sit, you and I don't have history."

Evie winced. *Because that organ in your chest is made of jagged stones.* Twelve years and his words still managed to stab like a dull blade, making it hard to take an easy breath. The frigid look in his rich-brown eyes registered crystal clear before he centered his attention back on the papers before him. It was the first time he'd shown sentiment of any kind directed at her. She bit the inside of her bottom lip to stifle the quiver of anger.

"I've reviewed Leonard's notes and think—" His head snapped up from the scribble. "Where are you going?"

"Have a nice life, Mr. Scott." A few short steps put her at the door, which she opened smoothly, contrary to the pumping agitation flickering her temper. She turned back to him, and the surprise that reflected in his eyes gave way to arrogance. "Or not. I don't care one way or the other."

Downstairs, she made her way back to Jasmine at the front desk while trying her best to maintain a professional mien despite her irritation building like lava boiling bursts of steam.

"Mrs. Powell, that was fast."

Evie turned her head to follow Jasmine's line of sight in the direction of the stairs.

"I'm waiting for Mr. Scott. He usually lets me know when to schedule your next appointment."

Don't hold your breath. She didn't expect he'd come running after her. He was as stubborn, exact, and self-righteous as he'd always been. "I won't be soliciting Mr. Scott or his firm's legal services. I'd like my jacket, please."

The young woman's head tilted to the side, as though she'd heard words she didn't understand. As if rejecting the illustrious Mr. Scott was unheard of. "My jacket," Evie repeated when Jasmine didn't move.

"Oh. Okay." She quickly retreated to the closet, then returned while glancing again in the direction of the stairs. "Well, I hope you have a nice day, Mrs. Powell."

"You, too."

Evie made it down to the lobby, heels hammering against the tile on her way to the exit, cursing herself for ever coming here.

Her Uber had an ETA of six minutes. As she impatiently waited, a black car came to a stop at the curb right in front of the building. In her haste to get the heck out of there, had she mistakenly selected an upgrade? She checked her phone. Behind her, the revolving door swirled, and out strode Vincent Scott with his cell phone to his ear and clutching that smart leather portfolio in his other hand. His stride slowed. The mere sight of him made her stomach drop. The steady blankness of his countenance, the look that always drummed up the guilt she carried, forced her to be the first to look away. The driver got out of the vehicle. Before he could make it around the car, Vincent opened the rear passenger-side door.

"Mrs. Powell."

With her attention centered on her phone, she didn't bother to acknowledge him. It wasn't in her nature to be cruel, but damn it, he provoked her.

Out of her periphery, she took note of Vincent's study of the white Toyota Corolla slowing behind the sleek black car before he folded himself inside, and his driver closed the door.

As she settled into the back seat of her own ride, she realized Vincent Scott was right about one thing: they didn't have history. Despite how nasty things ended between them, the callous individual she now encountered wasn't the man she'd met and spent her entire summer falling hard over. Her first love. First lover. He was no longer the man who she'd freely given a chunk of her soul. A vital piece she had yet to reclaim.

Chapter Two

CHASE CONFECTIONS WAS packed, practically every table occupied.

Evie kept a direct path to the counter. She'd left Vincent's office and came straight to the bakery, looking forward to working off the stress his mere presence spurred.

Laughter rang out, drawing her attention to the party of twelve lounging on the pale pink leather seating. The white plexiglass round table they were seated at held beverages, sandwiches, and an array of desserts.

The bakery boutique, as Kennedi's late mother coined it, had only reopened in its new location a little over a month ago and had nearly tripled in square footage. It stayed busy from opened to closed. Occupying space on the popular D.C. Wharf almost guaranteed high foot traffic.

The fact that the boutique was located mere steps from Shaw Hotel and Casino, which also recently had its grand opening, the new hotspot drew a lot of business the bakery's way.

"Hi, Amy. You're good here?" Evie asked the storefront supervisor while peeling out of her trench coat. A few minutes alone to breathe and clear her head were essential. She regarded the other three staffers at their registers. Each had quite a few patrons waiting in line, but orders were being filled rather quickly. "I can send someone from the kitchen to help out."

"No need. We're good. LaToya and Dani should be back from break any minute." Amy glanced away from her register. "Ooh, love the shoes. You look nice."

"Thanks." Promoting Amy to be storefront manager had been a smart choice. "Come get me if it starts to get crazy."

Evie pushed past the swinging door and crossed the wide corridor to the kitchen, which was just as busy as the front. She raised her voice over the clink of pans and working appliances. "Afternoon, everyone." Kennedi and Tabitha— her best friends and business partners—swiveled their heads. Tabitha's presence came as a bit of a surprise. "I'll be in the office." She continued down the hall, in desperate need of that minute to breathe. Her friends' light footfalls fell in pace behind her.

Please, one minute…two, tops.

She hung up her coat and sat behind the desk. With eyes closed and her head resting back against the chair, she released long, deep, even breaths, in and out, over and over, her fingers working her throbbing temples. "One. Two. Three…"

"Oh no, she's doing her serenity relaxation technique. That can't be good," Kennedi remarked, standing just inside the door.

Evie peeled an eyelid up to see them move to the front of the desk, then continued her breathing.

"Nope, not good," Tabitha said. "Tell us how the meeting went."

"It didn't." On a last long release, Evie opened her eyes. "Shouldn't you be home resting?" Tabitha had been on solid bedrest for four of her five and half months of pregnancy. Having endured ovarian cancer and subsequently lost a baby, her doctor was being extremely cautious.

"I had my checkup this morning and received the okay to return to work—"

"Part-time," Kennedi made clear.

"Yes, ma'am." Tabitha stroked her baby mound, the immense joy of becoming a mom glinting in her hazel eyes. "I've been advised to work half days. I left my doctor's office and came straight here. Lying around got old after the first week."

Evie yanked opened a desk drawer, followed by another. "Shit, where is it? There was a leftover bottle of Cabernet Franc your husband stuck in here following the boutique's grand opening. Dominic mentioned it to me."

"Trent and I killed that about a week ago," Kennedi said.

Evie and Tabitha gaped, then Evie frowned. She looked around the moderate-sized office and ended at the couch. "Please tell me you two didn't have sex in here."

"What?" Kennedi gasped. Her brow furrowed. "Of course not."

"Of course not!" Tabitha clutched her phantom pearls as she mocked her friend's ridiculous look. "Kenni, don't act brand-new. You and Trent had sex in the kitchen of our old bakery, so you two getting busy in this office wouldn't be much of a stretch."

Kennedi cut a grin. "Touché, but for the record, Trent and I decided a month ago to abstain from sex until our wedding. We've stuck to it. And Saturday cannot come fast enough," she muttered, and they laughed. "To say it's been a long month is putting it mildly."

"No doubt it has for you two," Tabitha teased. "But I can relate. Dominic and I didn't have sex throughout my entire first trimester. He was fearful of complications with the baby. We've since made up for it." She smiled, her eyes mischievously bright, deservingly happy. "Now the man can't keep his hands to himself."

One month for Kennedi. A trimester for Tabitha. *Try over a year and a half for me.*

Evie listened to the ladies as they chatted about their spouses, who also happened to be brothers. She was thrilled her two best friends had found their soul mates but a bit envious, too.

"I'll come by tonight to get Dixie and Percy," Tabitha said on her way to the couch, stretching out her frame. "I miss my babies."

"Okay." Evie had enjoyed having the little furry friends to come home to.

"Well, are you going to tell us how it went today with the new attorney?" Kennedi asked.

"I told you it didn't. The guy was getting carted off to an ambulance when I arrived."

"Oh no!" Kennedi gaped.

Tabitha sat up. "What happened?"

"Not sure. Stroke, maybe. He looked super pale and sweaty, that's all I know." She slipped into a pair of flats that Kennedi kept tucked underneath the desk. "His client list was split among the partners. And guess who got my case?

Yep, not-so-lucky me," she drawled, easily reading their tense faces. "Apparently, Vincent Scott is the best at handling 'messy divorces'—" she made hard air quotes "—like mine. He was so damned smug, too. I terminated the firm's services. I don't need nor want to deal with him."

"Evie, I understand you and Vincent have some bad blood, but maybe you could set your differences aside," Kennedi suggested. "Trent says Vincent is a killer attorney. You want to get your divorce taken care of, don't you?"

"Trent's biased. He and Vincent are friends. I wouldn't want my loser ex-boyfriend anywhere near me," Tabitha remarked, always the pragmatist. That tiny diamond stud at the right side of her nose glinted against the fluorescent overhead lighting. "Evie, steer clear of him."

"It's about business." Kennedi didn't let up. "She needs a good attorney, and Vincent can fulfill that role."

"Kennedi, get real," Tabitha argued. "Vincent just up and walked away from Evie when they were dating without so much as a screw you."

"It wasn't quite like that. We both had—" Evie started.

"Sometimes you have to put feelings aside," Kennedi cut in.

Tabitha shook her head. "I disagree. She did right to terminate his legal services. You shouldn't have suggested Vincent's firm in the first place." She turned her head to Evie from her position on the couch. "Girlfriend, there are other good attorneys out there. Vincent isn't the be-all and end-all."

Evie agreed, but… "Finding a good one in this city who isn't backlogged is the issue. Maybe Mr. Sigler will take me back. He was slow to act, but I just need to be patient."

"No, keep looking," Tabitha asserted in her usual direct manor. "He had you waiting six months."

"On a different topic, Evie—you understand that if I had a choice, I wouldn't have put Vincent in my wedding. Sistahood first. But he's Trent's close friend," Kennedi told her.

"It's fine. He's the one who acts as though I don't exist whenever we're in the same room. Oh, and we never had a history. That's what he said to me. Can you believe that!"

"Really?" Kennedi frowned.

"Dom said Vincent might be bringing a date," Tabitha remarked casually.

Evie's spine straightened. She looked at Kennedi. "He has a date?"

"He asked Trent if it'd be okay, given that it's last-minute and all."

She wished it didn't affect her, but damn it, it did.

A knock came at the door. Kennedi opened it. "John, hi." She hugged Tabitha's eldest brother.

"Hey, ladies. I was told I'd find the three of you holding court in here."

He crossed the room to Tabitha and gave her a hug. "Baby sis, what are you doing here? Shouldn't you be in bed?"

"I'm back part-time."

"And my nephew? All good?" A hint of caution filtered into his tone as he rested a hand atop her baby bump.

It'd been announced about a week ago Tabitha was having a boy. Evie wanted to throw her friend a gender-reveal party, but Tabitha wouldn't hear of it. She considered it a ridiculous waste of time and money.

"He's good. We're good. What brings you by?"

"I came to see Evie."

Tall, muscular, and gorgeous, John Seils was pleasant eye candy. His smooth, sun-kissed, tawny-brown skin proved he spent his days working outdoors.

Like Tabitha's dark mane that she kept in a long single braid, her brother had a head of lustrously wavy, raven locks that hit his shoulders. Seldom did Evie see it out of a hair band. Whiskey-gold eyes beneath thick, dark brows, prominent cheekbones and a sharp jawline, the man was smoking hot.

Evie rounded the desk, and John gave her a hug. The big bulk of his upper body swaddled her in warmth before he pulled an envelope from his back pocket and handed it to her.

"I was in the area and thought I'd drop off your invoice. A couple things to note. The pool's uncovered and filled. I left the heater on to make sure everything's functioning as it should. It's programmed to shut off around eight tonight. I'm afraid the lining in the water garden had to be fully replaced. The rip was clean through, beyond repair. But there's no charge." He tilted his head at the envelope. "Everything's spelled out."

"John, I saw the mess that pond was in. Add the cost to your invoice."

He waved her off. "Don't worry about it. It's all taken care of. I've put you on a biweekly maintenance schedule. Two of my guys will see to things. Come winter, they'll turn off the pumps before the first frost to prevent the pipes from bursting. That's what tore the lining."

The landscape around her home had gotten out of control. John's company typically did commercial design and install. But as his sister's friend, he'd made an exception for Evie.

"Thanks. The place was beginning to look like a jungle."

"No problem." His handsome grin stretched to the glint in his eyes. "I should get going."

Evie smiled back. A sudden replay of the afternoon with Vincent filled her head space. And he'd be bringing a date this weekend. He wouldn't be alone. Well, she didn't need to be either. "John," she called out. "I know this is extremely short notice. Kennedi's wedding is this Saturday. I was wondering if you'd join me?"

Crinkles marred his smooth brow. A small curve spread across his lips. "Join you? As in a date?"

She was so damn rusty at this. Kennedi and Tabitha's profiles registered in her periphery. Both wore gaping stares. She stepped over to John—not that lowering her voice would prevent the ladies from listening in. "As my plus-one. If you're seeing someone… I probably should've asked before… I-I mean—"

"Yes, I'll be your plus-one."

That white-toothed grin of his crept a bit wider. And his answer didn't necessarily confirm he wasn't seeing someone. Given her life circumstances, that was good enough for her. "I'll text you the particulars. I'm part of the wedding party and must get there early. You'll have to meet me at the venue."

"Not a problem." He glanced at the ladies, then back at her. "Saturday then."

When the door closed, Evie turned and tried to ignore their fixed gawks. She went to the locker in the corner and stripped out of her dress.

"Evie, what are you doing?"

"Changing my clothes to get to work." She knew it wasn't what Kennedi was referring to, but she needed a moment to conjure up an answer. Her actions with John had been spontaneous at best but no less ill-advised.

"Tell me you didn't just asked John out."

Unable to deny it, she turned and met Kennedi's accusatory glower as she brought up her jeans over her hips and grabbed a Chase Confections signature pale pink T-shirt. "John has asked me out before, but I've always said no. What's the difference in me asking him and him saying yes?"

"Because you and I know the difference is you only asked him to show up Vincent. Besides, you've been pretty adamant about not seeing anyone while you're still considered legally married." Kennedi turned to Tabitha. "He's your brother. Tell her it's not cool."

Tabitha eased up from the couch and stretched her arms above her head, rolling her shoulders. "John's thirty-four, a big boy. He can take care of himself. But, Evie, that's not like you." She strode to the door; opened it. "I'm impressed. It's about time," she uttered on her way out.

Evie could always count on her girl, Tab, to be exact, no-nonsense.

She delivered Kennedi—who narrow-eyed her—a firm nod. "There. See? No big deal."

Chapter Three

MINGLED CONVERSATIONS CARRIED high-pitched voices, all of them competing with the pounding music. Since its opening day, the Reef—Shaw Hotel and Casino's rotating rooftop bar and lounge—had easily become the go-to hotspot in D.C., despite the high-dollar menu and top-tier spirits.

Six to eight hundred dollars reserved a waterfront view of one of the forty or so deep, cushioned couches and double-wide chairs beneath crisp white canopy curtains. The private seating lined the plexiglass guardrail on all four sides of the building and offered a nice panorama of the Wharf's skyline.

The evening temperature had dropped a few degrees. Chilly enough to draw everyone indoors, but several strategically placed firepits kept the open-air bar bathed in cozy warmth.

As Vincent discussed over the phone with his assistant a few items for next week's court appearance, he cut through the throng congregating practically shoulder to shoulder, keeping a narrow path to where he knew his buddy would be. Trenton Shaw, the man whose surname was illuminated in electric blue on the forty-story tower beneath Vincent's feet. Its triton logo silhouette rode the side of the building, guiding those seeking high-stakes nightlife entertainment.

"No bachelor party." Trenton had been adamant on that front, but his brother, Dominic, wouldn't let up, so the brothers had settled on a meet-up for drinks.

Vincent took a moment to talk through a couple more directives with his assistant. He paused a moment, lips quirked, and shook his head as he watched the waitress approach and croon over Trenton before jotting down Dominic's order of a bison burger with all the fixings to accompany his Maker's Mark. The man's six-two frame was all lean, solid muscle, yet he consumed food like a linebacker.

Before Vincent could put his phone away, another call chimed. The number displayed indicated a work matter that would take far more time than he wanted to give to it at present. He stuck the phone in the front pocket of his slacks while contemplating whether to turn the damn thing off.

"And you, sir?" The waitress grabbed his attention.

"Pappy Van Winkle. Neat," Trenton answered before Vincent could reply.

Vincent grinned. "What he said."

Still wearing that starry-eyed smile, she went on her way.

"I see you have a fan. Several in fact," Vincent told him as their palms met and they pulled in with bro hugs. He noticed there were many patrons' eyes aimed at the hotel-casino mogul, who didn't seem at all fazed. The ladies didn't stand a chance. For one, Trenton's personal security was seated casually, unassumingly, a short distance away. And two, Trenton was getting married tomorrow to Kennedi Avery Chase, the love of his life. His buddy had been walking around in a love-induced, dreamy daze for months.

"You're missing a groomsman. Where's your cousin?"

Fine grooves dented Trenton's brow. "I left Eaton a message, told him where we'd be. He had better not fuck up tomorrow."

"I'll kick his ass if he does." Dominic stepped forward. "Vin, my man, how's it going?" They gripped hands, and pulled in.

"All good." Vincent sank into the thick cushions and let go a long, weary breath.

"Busy day?" Trenton asked.

"Try busy week. Court ran long, only for my motion to be overturned. I had a colleague suffer a heart attack at the office yesterday. I just received an update from my assistant on his condition."

"No shit?" Dominic sat up. "Did he make it?"

"He had to have three stents. I see the guy in the gym regularly. He's in his mid-thirties."

"Damn, around our age." Trenton shook his head.

"My partners and I took over his client list. Evie Powell's case was among them." Vincent rotated and stroked the rock of tension at the back of his neck, the mental weight of responsibilities bearing down heavier lately. "Evie arrived to meet with Rosati just as he was being rolled out."

"Tell me you're not taking her case."

Trenton's incredulity was justified. The brothers knew about Vincent's past involvement with Evie. "She fired me. We had words."

Trenton raised an eyebrow. "What sort of words?"

"It's not important." He shifted around, feeling stretched taut within his skin. Talk of Evie always left him vexed and edgy and strangely unable to keep a clear head. That drink couldn't come fast enough.

"The world is pretty damn small," Dominic remarked. "What are the odds Trent would marry a woman who happens to be best friends with the woman you once had hard feelings for?"

"Yeah, I should play the damn lottery," Vincent scoffed.

"Think about it. You told us that you and Evie met one summer in Connecticut. Then, over a decade later, you both unknowingly end up here in D.C. And now Trent's about to marry Kennedi, Evie's best friend. Something could be said about that. I don't know, stars aligning or some shit."

"It means my luck isn't worth shit," Vincent ground out, happy to see the waitress approaching with his order. The second the glass filled his palm, he gulped it to near empty and put in for a second.

"You handled the joint venture between Shaw Hotel and Casino and Chase Confections last year. How could you not have run into Evie?" Dominic questioned between a bite of his burger.

"Dude, do you know how many client acquisitions I have on my desk? They're all just case numbers to me." Staying impassive helped Vincent effectively do his job. "In any event, Evie and Tabitha each own twenty-five percent of Chase. My focus was on taking down the decision-maker on Trent's behalf, Kennedi Chase. I would've been successful, too." He cut a grin at Trenton. "But this one here decided to fall in love with her."

Trenton smiled. "I like to think I came out on the winning end."

Dominic came to his feet and raised his glass. "A toast to my brother for getting it right the second time around." With drinks in hand, Vincent and Trenton joined him, clinking their glasses. All humor left Dominic's features as he brought a solid hand down on his brother's shoulder. "Really, bro, Kennedi is a terrific lady."

"Definitely," Vincent added. "I'm happy for you, my brother."

They sat and chatted in between another round of drinks while watching threads of warm bodies gyrate on the over-crowded dance floor several yards away. A couple of hours later, it was only Vincent and Trenton. Dominic had left for home to see to his pregnant wife.

"So, Evie fired you." Trenton looked at him.

Over twelve years, yet Vincent remembered every minute detail about her. His mind refused to let him forget what it felt like to caress the delicateness of her skin. The soft green flecks of her eyes, with depths that always distracted him. The silky glide of her lips against his. How she would bat his hand away when he'd teasingly count the cute brush of freckles across the bridge of her nose. Whenever he encountered Evie, he did his best to keep his gaze elsewhere, to not stare. And whenever she left an area, the enticing scent, a delicate balance of fresh and sweet, lingered a moment before dissipating. He'd experienced it in his office yesterday.

"What's on your mind?"

Vincent blinked, coming out of his musings, and snatched the glass from the table. He resented how she was still able to affect him after so much time had passed.

"I read over Rosati's notes on Evie's case..." Though

he'd been *fired*, attorney-client privilege still applied. He swirled the dark liquid in his glass and met Trenton's inquisitive blue-eyed stare. "I would've expected she'd do better, that's all."

"Sometimes we get it wrong the first time."

His buddy was speaking from experience. Trenton was walking into his second marriage tomorrow. It was Vincent who'd helped unshackle the guy from his first.

"The outfits. The hair. Cherry-colored lipstick. Smelling good. I think the damn woman does it on purpose."

Trenton reared back. "So, you think Evie makes herself attractive to spite you?" He laughed deep in his throat. "That's about the most ridiculous thing I've ever heard."

Vincent brought up his glass to his lips, but Trenton snatched it and set it on the table out of easy reach. "Dude, I was drinking that."

"You've officially hit the wall." Trenton pressed the table remote and raised a hand, signaling for the waitress. "You're cut off, my friend. I need you standing upright tomorrow."

It was indeed a foolish thing to say. Vincent wasn't sure where exactly he was going with the argument. He could hold his own, but given his lack of sleep, his head was beginning to feel a bit lopsided. Still… "All I'm saying is, I think she tries to get under my skin."

The waitress stepped beneath the canopy. "I'd like to close out," Trenton told her.

"It's on the house, Mr. Shaw." Her smile was near blinding as she gazed back at the guy.

"Thanks, but I'd like the bill, if you don't mind," Vincent requested. She quickly trotted to the bar, then returned and handed over the billfold. He signed a well-deserved two-hundred-and-fifty-dollar gratuity. He'd watched her scurry about from partygoer to partygoer all evening. Bussing tables, washing dishes until dawn, and sweeping floors had once been his life. He understood the grind. "I appreciate you taking care of us tonight."

"It was my pleasure. If there's anything else you need, just tap the button." She pointed at the built-in table device. "Gentlemen, enjoy the rest of your night."

Trenton sat back. "Obviously, Evie gets under your skin because you have unresolved issues with her."

Vincent exhaled heavily. "Man, I can't even explain it. I was addicted to that woman. I'm talking crazy hooked. I asked her to marry me," he confided in his friend, whom he'd known since that summer their Scout troops met during a hiking retreat in the hills of the Great Smoky Mountains and had shared a bond with ever since. "She was Evie Langston when I knew her. Beautiful. Smart. Funny. And interested in a guy like me, a greasy-ass mechanic, who just happened to pull the short straw in Joe's garage that rainy night."

"You fixed her car? So that's how you two met. You never volunteered the details, so I didn't ask."

"Not much to tell. A beautiful woman gets stalled on the side of the road. I towed her car to Joe's garage. We hit it off and ended up spending that entire summer together. The night before she was due to return to Brown, she asked if I'd ever considered going to college. I told her I'd dropped out a year before, that it wasn't for me." Vincent sighed long again, rotating his shoulders, the stress of the day settling in his bones. "I'll just say my wanting to take a different path—work with my hands instead of using my brain, as she saw it—" his lips thinned "—was beneath Miss Ivy League."

Trenton's eyes widened a touch then narrowed. "Really? Evie said that?" He sounded skeptical.

"Her father went to West Point, and her mother is a Brown alumnus. They're her adopted parents. A white couple. Her mother wasn't thrilled about us dating. I believe it was because my family didn't come from their little Fairfield County bubble—you know, opposite sides of the track, that and the fact that I was a mechanic."

"Did she say that?"

"Not in so many words. Her father…he was never rude but didn't say much. Maybe he felt the same. Who the hell knows? What I do know is they had expectations. All Evie ever talked about was setting high goals and achieving. Simply put, I didn't fit the mode. She dropped me and kept it moving. The life direction I wanted to take wasn't good enough—I wasn't good enough, at least not beyond a summer."

Trenton stared at him for a moment. "I've only known Evie a short time, but I don't see the self-absorbed person you've depicted. At any rate, she was young. Ambitious. You can't fault her for that."

"Yes, well, she married some dude from a well-to-do family, who she's now divorcing." Vincent chuckled, still feeling the bitter residual of her slight. "Talk about karma."

"Yet, you managed to accomplish all the things she envisioned for you," Trenton pointed out, giving him a side look.

"It had nothing to do with her."

"Joe losing his garage in the fire and getting taken advantage of in the lawsuit…what happened to him was horrible. I know it motivated you to pursue your law degree. But can you honestly say somewhere deep down, Evie didn't play a small part?"

He could see he wasn't going to get any sympathy from his friend.

"All I'm saying is bridges have been mended for far less serious crimes," Trenton said.

Vincent snatched his glass and tipped it back, emptying its contents, then pushed up from the couch, ready to call it a night. "It's called the past for a reason," he muttered on their way out.

At home, following a hot shower, with his notepad and several case files spread out over his bed, Vincent set the TV channel to *Shark Tank*, then grabbed the first of several folders.

The digital clock on the bedside table showed 9:47 p.m. Pillows fluffed, he situated himself against the headboard, prepped to get in a few hours of notetaking before shutting down for the night. His cell phone buzzed somewhere among the papers. As he shuffled the pile around, Evie Powell's business card—Chase Confections in hot pink embossed lettering—slipped out of the heap. Rosati had written her home address and cell phone number on the back. Vincent did a quick internet map search and discovered they lived only a neighborhood apart. "Stars aligned" according to Dominic.

He placed the card on the nightstand, not sure why he'd

taken it before having his assistant archive her file. The phone buzzed again, demanding his attention. He read his sister's text.

We're set on the cake, right?

"Shit." He'd forgotten to place the order with Chase Confections for her graduation cake. Sasha had worked her butt off, took summer and winter classes to be able to graduate from American University an entire year early.

He replied:

The party isn't for several weeks. We have plenty of time.

You haven't ordered it yet! Chase Confections books months in advance. I know you're busy. I'll take care of it.

She was right. The popular bakery tended to have a long waiting list when it came to their custom cake designs. Knowing the owners had to count in his favor. He hoped.

I'll handle it. I promise.

That's what you said weeks ago.

I got it covered. You just keep your guest list to thirty.

Not expecting a reply—Sasha's way of plausible deniability—he set the phone on the table and dived into his work. His mind drifted to Evie Powell again, a subliminal pull. The sudden desire to call her rode his conscience.

She'd fired him. He'd acted unprofessionally and deserved it. If nothing else, she was owed an apology. He retrieved her card from the table along with his phone and tapped in her number. After a string of rings, it went to voicemail. He didn't leave a message. They weren't on the best of terms. Far from it. It would have been more surprising had she answered. And yet, he couldn't shake the gnawing urgency to simply hear her voice.

Chapter Four

IT WAS HER friend's big day. The strapless, white satin gown flowed fluidly along Kennedi's lean figure. Her hair, a relaxed ponytail banded at the nape. Soft beach-wave curls framed her lovely oval face.

"Kennedi, you look so beautiful." Evie stood beside her at the full-length mirror. She grabbed an extra sparkly hairpin to secure the delicate tulle veil at the back of Kennedi's head.

"You really do." Alizka—Lizzie—Kennedi's future sister-in-law, bent to assist Kennedi into her white satin pumps.

"Gorgeous," Tabitha agreed from her view in the chair.

While the makeup artist had piled on foundation to hide Evie's freckles and offered a bit of warmth to her otherwise fair-brown skin, Kennedi wore only a touch of cover-up. The natural beauty of her flawless, toffee-brown shade practically shimmered.

"Let's take a picture." Tabitha got up a bit awkwardly. The flowy, violet chiffon bridesmaid's dress succeeded in softening the severe roundness of her belly. She retrieved the bridal bouquet of white calla lilies from the coffee table, handed it to Kennedi, then took out her cell phone. They huddled close, laughing heartily as she snapped several shots, some with their tongues poking out, others with rabbit-ear gestures over Kennedi's head.

A knock came at the door. Marie, the wedding coordinator, poked her head inside. "We're seven minutes behind schedule and still down one groomsman. It's…" She looked at her electronic pad. "Eaton. But no fear. I'm told he's on his way. Are we all good here?"

"We're fine," Kennedi said, appearing fully composed.

"Terrific. I'll be back shortly." The door closed.

"This is it." Kennedi smiled, her warm brown eyes glistening. "Thank you for being here with me."

"Don't you dare cry. You'll ruin your face." Tabitha snatched a tissue from the box on the table and carefully touched it to the inner corners of Kennedi's eyes. "You're going to make me cry, which lately, I apparently do at the drop of a hat." Their attention returned to the door when it opened once more.

"Kennedi—" Georgina Balaska Shaw, her soon-to-be mother-in-law, stopped short. "My dear, don't you look lovely." She approached, palmed and kissed Kennedi's cheek, then turned to Tabitha, her other daughter-in-law. "In less than four months, I'll be a grandmother. My boys have done me proud with you two." Her red-painted lips started to tremble. "I couldn't be happier than I am in this very moment."

"Mom, no crying." Alizka snagged another tissue and handed it off to her mother. "You and Kennedi are going to have racoon eyes before the ceremony even begins."

A knock sounded, then the door to the sitting room opened yet again. Marie entered. "Eaton has arrived. We can start."

"I'll go take my place. That's of course after I remove Harold from it." The scowl that twisted Mrs. Shaw's face stole the warmth from her blue eyes. "He has some nerve," she grumbled on her way out.

Evie asked Kennedi, "Who's Harold?"

"My dad," Alizka answered. "Well, he's Trent's dad, but he raised me since I was a baby. He arrived this morning. My parents don't necessarily see eye to eye on much."

"We really should get started. We're twenty-three minutes off schedule," the ever-efficient wedding coordinator said amid ushering them to the door. "Ladies, the men are waiting. Kennedi, you'll stay back until I give the signal."

Out in the hall, Mrs. Shaw was chatting with the groomsmen. Marie did her best to work around the meddle-some intrusion, herding everyone into their places as the music procession started.

With Tabitha and Dominic leading the train, Evie took her place next to Trenton's cousin, Eaton, at the rear. She delivered a glance at Vincent, who merely did the same as he came to stand next to Alizka.

"Marie, this just won't do." Mrs. Shaw tapped her chin, eyeing the wedding party. "Eaton, you'll pair with Lizzie." She tugged him out of the orderly lineup. "Vincent, you and Evie are the tallest." She moved them about, refitting her puzzle pieces. "Well now, don't you two make a lovely picture. Wait..." A few unruly curls that escaped Evie's carefully arranged low bun became Mrs. Shaw's next target. "Here, let me fix—"

"Mom, really? We need to get moving." Alizka shooed

her away.

"Okay, okay, I'm going." She scurried out.

"Aren't you glad we got married in Vegas?" Tabitha muttered to Dominic and entwined her arm with his.

"Wait until the baby comes," Dominic returned. "The overattentive Greek grandmother will be in full form."

They all laughed.

Vincent proffered his bent arm. "Mrs. Powell."

He was smooth-shaven and smelled of a pleasant cologne. *He's so damn attractive.* Evie schooled her expression from betraying any reaction. "Mr. Scott." As she slipped her arm around the bulk of muscle, she could almost feel the twine of tension rolling off him.

Marie gave the signal. Dominic, with Tabitha at his side, headed off, followed by Alizka and Eaton. When it was Evie's turn, she glanced up to find deep brown eyes, somewhat hooded, focused on her. That look, the familiar, all-encompassing stare that used to make her melt, brought out of nowhere a molten desire that prompted a flush of heat to her face.

His slight tug and stride forward got her head back in the game. They made their way down the aisle. When they separated and took their places at the front of the crowd of family and friends, she took a steadying breath. A small part of her wanted to hold on to that remembered feeling that once tethered them.

Which one is she? Evie scanned the many lovely faces, wondering who Vincent's companion was this evening. The fact that he had several admirers staring his way made it a challenge. Her gaze landed on her handsome plus-one. John smiled back at her with a slight nod. She returned the gesture, then stole a look at Vincent. His stare, deep, serious, was once again pinned on her. His eyes slowly shifted in John's direction, then returned to her.

Thankfully, the wedding march began. Kennedi, with a sure hold on her father's arm, started down the aisle, drawing everyone's undivided attention. Her father's ongoing struggle with dementia made it difficult to really know his mental state in this moment, but his presence meant the world to Kennedi. Evie took note of the nurse seated on the front row who rose to assist Mr. Chase to his seat beside her as Kennedi continued forward.

Throughout the ceremony, Evie felt as though she was being watched. Vincent held her in intense scrutiny. When it was time to pair up again to take their walk back down the aisle, just before she and Vincent broke away, his warm fingers swept over hers resting at the bend of his arm, for the barest of moments.

What am I to make of that?

THE SLIDE OF chairs across the smooth tile resonated as guests rose to their feet for a standing ovation. Whoops and cheers rang out as Kennedi and Trenton concluded their first dance as husband and wife.

Vincent cut around people and tables to stand behind Tabitha and Dominic. Both were holding separate conversations with guests. He took note of their entwined fingers and how Dominic's thumb administered slow brushstrokes across his wife's knuckles, no doubt an unconscious, affectionate gesture as he debated with the man on his right about the Nats' win from last night. Beside Dominic, Tabitha looked all but expressionless as the woman before her went on and on about a recipe that "would surely be a hit." When the woman caught the sleeve of another poor soul to torment, Vincent eased into the vacancy. He smiled at Tabitha.

"Everyone's a pastry genius."

"They like to think so." She gave a slight smile. "Enjoying yourself?"

He looked around at the two hundred or so guests dancing and having a good time. "Beautiful couple, beautiful wedding, beautiful night—it's hard not to. By the way, I hear you're no longer on bedrest. Congrats."

"Thank you." A soft smile filled her tawny features as she stroked the perfect roundness of her stomach.

"I hate to disrupt the mood of the evening by discussing a work matter, but I was wondering if I could ask a favor." She tipped her head, so he went on. "I'm throwing my sister, Sasha, a graduation party and…"

"You'd like Chase Confections to cater the desserts. Graduations, proms, weddings…it's that time of year. Orders have been flooding in for weeks."

"I'd assumed as much. Actually, what I'm looking for is a custom cake. According to Sasha, Kennedi had agreed some time ago to create a graduation cake. My sister acts as though the words were carved in stone. In any case, I know Kennedi and Trent will be away on their honeymoon. I'd intended to put the order in a long time ago, but it slipped my mind."

"We're pretty booked. We typically require at least three

months' advance notice. That said, what exactly are you looking to have done? Depending on the complexity and when you'll need it, I might be able to assign one of our junior pastry chefs to handle it."

"About a month from now. Sasha would like a cake shaped in her likeness, wearing her cap and gown. I'm not sure the height or how large. Her guest list is limited to thirty, but I suspect there will be a few more."

"There always are."

Vincent expected she'd call out the ridiculousness of his tardy request. Instead, she nodded as if he'd asked for a simple cupcake. He'd seen what the ladies could do at Chase Confections. They were masters at their craft. But still… "I understand if you don't have the availability."

"Availability for what?" Dominic turned and slipped an arm around his wife's waist, drawing her intimately close.

"A custom cake for his sister," Tabitha explained. "With the short turnaround, something that elaborate would require myself or one of my partners to design it," she said to Vincent. "Actually, Evie's the best among us at sculpting facial likenesses."

They both looked across the ballroom at Evie dancing with the man she'd been hemmed to all evening. Vincent tried to keep his vexed emotions out of his face, but Tabitha's right eyebrow lifted, a sure sign he'd failed.

"I'm aware of the animosity between you two. But with Kennedi about to go on her honeymoon and me working a reduced schedule, Evie's your best bet. Considering our calendar is full, she'd be doing you a huge favor to move you to the top of the orders and would have to put in extra time to fulfill your request."

Vincent looked at Dominic and received a shrug. He'd learned a long time ago the man's wife never minced words. She came direct. Always. "I hear you. Thanks."

Arm in arm, the couple strolled on.

Sasha is going to murder me.

That damn cake had been the only gift she'd asked of him.

He crossed the room and planted himself at the bar. "My man, I'll have a Dewar's, neat."

"Sure thing. I got you next after the gentleman there."

To Vincent's right stood the man he knew to be Evie's date. Dark hair slicked back into a ponytail. Muscles bulged in the well-cut gray suit. The guy looked to be about the same height as him—a little over six feet two. They were close in skin color. Well, if Vincent had time to get out of the office before the sun went down, maybe get back to running outdoors, he too, would sport a nice, rich golden brown. *Why the fuck am I sizing him up?* He delivered a nod and received the same before the man accepted the two drinks the bartender handed him. Vincent tracked him back over to Evie and read the intimate closeness as the two sat side by side. The happy couple.

Fuck.

"Here you go, sir."

In much need of the scotch, he downed a good bit with one swallow and turned his head just in time to witness the man lean in at Evie's ear. Whatever was said brought a subtle curve to her pretty mouth and an instant flush to the plump upswept angles of her cheeks. Why should he care? But he did. It'd been twelve years. Why did she still affect his psyche?

Just then, both stood up and moved to the dance floor where they'd been from the moment the reception kicked off. Vincent remembered how much Evie enjoyed dancing. It'd been what they'd often—

A hand smacked against his back, startling him. He snapped his head around. "Dom."

"You're flying solo tonight? I thought you were bringing a date."

"Changed my mind." Vincent shifted his gaze back to Evie. Alongside the apology he owed her and now having to ask her to create a cake, he'd hoped… Shit, he wasn't sure what the hell he'd thought would happen tonight between them. "Who's the dude?" He angled his chin over at Evie dancing with her companion. "You know him?"

"Ah." Dominic grinned. "You still have the feels for that lady, don't you?"

He didn't admit or deny, which in itself was an admission Evie still had a residual hold on him, one that not even he understood. Vincent gulped what was left in his glass in an attempt to dispel the complexities of his thoughts. "Either you know him or you don't. Which is it?"

"Are you asking for a friend?" Dominic chuckled but sobered quickly beneath Vincent's narrowed side-eye. "He's my brother-in-law, John Seils. The man has some moves…and good game apparently."

"What does he do?"

"Landscaping. You've seen my property. Best in the neighborhood."

"He cuts grass for living." Vincent snorted.

Dominic grinned. "No. His company does landscape design and maintenance for commercial new construction. You're familiar with that huge business and residential complex going up over in Springfield?" Getting a nod, Dominic said, "Seils Landscaping won the bid. He has his staff tend to my grounds only because I'm married to his sister. John and I didn't hit it off at first. But once he realized I was serious about Tabitha, he came around."

"So, they're dating?"

"It's the first I've seen them together. The guy's pretty cool. Anyway, it's good to see Evie enjoying herself. From what I know that husband of hers is a real dick."

Vincent turned his attention to Evie again, feeling the need to keep her in his line of sight. Trenton stepped in the way, heading toward him.

"There's the man of the hour," Dominic bellowed and pulled his brother into a hug.

Vincent gave his buddy, who'd been smiling wide all night, the same celebratory greeting. "Congrats again, my friend."

"I'm a lucky man." Trenton looked at his wife across the room as she made her rounds, chatting with each guest. "Damn lucky."

"I'll drink to that." Dominic put in an order of shots that were quickly poured and slid over. They tapped their glasses and tossed back the dark bourbon.

An abrupt break in the music brought the entire festivities to a halt.

"What is Mom up to?" Dominic nudged his brother as

they observed their mother, with a drink in one hand, grab the wireless mic from the DJ's mixing board with the other. She tapped the tip of a nude-painted nail atop the device, then her voice reverberated through the surround sound. "One two, one two. Hi, everyone…"

"Oh, shit!" Trenton shrunk back. "Please tell me she's not about to sing."

"I'm so glad I got hitched in Vegas." Dominic laughed and looked around. "Where's the videographer? I hope she's getting this. I want a copy."

"Oof." Trenton flinched. "What's in that drink? It's not like Mom to show herself."

"I think it's because Dad's here. They've been at each other's throats since he arrived this morning. She's worked up."

"Has to be."

Vincent listened to the guys as Georgina Shaw went on about how she'd raised Trenton from the age of five, her immense love for him, and how Trenton turned his father's down-and-out business into an empire. She didn't spare her feelings about how, after she and Trenton's father, who was standing but a short distance away and wearing an expression of objection, divorced, that she was fortunate to remain Trenton's mother. She extended her drink hand to Kennedi and blew a kiss. As her speech started in on her love for her new daughter-in-law, her eyes welled. Vincent contained his smirk. "Yeah, your mother might be a little on edge…but also a bit juiced."

"In celebration of the bride and groom, let's have the wedding party join them in a dance," Georgina announced.

"It's tradition."

"Since when?" Harold Shaw asked her, still sporting his scowl of discontent.

"Since now," Georgina hissed low back at her ex-husband, then smiled brightly at the guests.

Kennedi, with Tabitha beside her, headed to their mother-in-law. Trenton and Dominic followed suit. Eaton cut through the crowd, as did Alizka.

Vincent stared back at Evie, who didn't move.

"We're missing a pair." Georgina narrowed in on Vincent at the bar. "And Evie, where are you? Ah, there you are. Come on, you two." She beckoned with her glass before directing the DJ to play something slow. The smooth, melodic tune geared up almost instantly.

Vincent came out of his lean against the bar's solid oak and strode over as Evie made her way forward, reluctance conveyed in her slothful stride. She came up to him. Eyes the beautiful color of young spring leaves behind dark winged lashes bored into him. "I guess we're doing this."

"Guess so." Delicate hands rested on his shoulders.

He slipped his arms around the small curve of her waist and was surprised when he didn't have to coax her closer. They fell into an easy swaying rhythm guided by the soft, sultry sounds flowing around them.

The scent of her, the feel of her, it was like a potent drug he'd once overcome but had easily reawakened. He closed his eyes for a moment, feeling like an addict taunted for a fix as he took the uniqueness that was only her deep into his lungs, then looked down at the beauty of her face. Makeup prevented him from counting her freckles, something he used to enjoy doing.

"Evie?" he called softly. Her radiant eyes fluttered up, meeting his. "I…" He glanced up to find John Seils staring directly at him, his features composed but no less imposing. Vincent brought his attention back to Evie. "A little piece of advice. Dating, or whatever it is you're doing while in the middle of divorce litigation proceedings, could hurt your case. You might want to practice discretion." That wasn't what he'd intended to say, but the harsh way her companion regarded him, cloaked behind an impassive mask, provoked Vincent's brain to take a left turn.

"I don't need your advice. I fired you, remember?"

"Oh, I haven't forgotten. I see that habit of yours hasn't changed."

"And I see you have selective amnesia." Her glare narrowed. "Look, I'm done with the sideways banter." Her voice was low but severe. "You disappear without so much as a text and now stand here as though I've wronged you. I'm not the one who walked away."

"You may as well have. I merely saved you the trouble." With teeth clenched yet maintaining his schooled demeanor as they battled it out in the center of the dance floor, he dropped his voice just above a whisper. "You made it clear what you thought of me."

"I only wanted to see you reach your full potential, which it seems you have. A mechanic—"

"Was beneath you." The soft melody rolled into a more upbeat tune and others joined the floor. Vincent released her and stepped back. "You can admit it."

"That's not—" she started.

"But you forget, *Mrs. Powell,* it was this mechanic who got you and your busted ignition coil off the side of the road."

"And that chip you've apparently been lugging around for twelve years must be pretty damn heavy by now. Enjoy your night, *Mr. Scott.*"

Chapter Five

*T*HE *DAMN NERVE.*

Evie marched off the dance floor and out onto the terrace. She sucked in the city's crisp evening breeze while pushing against her raw desire to go back in there and slap his smug face. His damn use of her married name was a condescending reminder of her life choice.

She filled her lungs once more, then let the air out slowly to draw a measure of calm. Her past swam around her much too fast, while the contentment of her future was taking far too long to come.

There was regret with how she'd handled things with Vincent those many years ago, but the blame could be shared, *damn it. He doesn't see the scars from the deep wounds he left behind.*

"Hey."

John came up beside her with a relaxed lean against the stone guardrail, facing her. Genuine concern blanketed his handsome features.

"Hey."

"You okay?"

"Yeah." She released another weary breath, far from okay. "Just tired."

"Your ex is back at the bar, drowning himself in premium-grade whiskey. Did I overdo it? I guess I don't know my own level of charm." His playful grin weakened. "From what I could tell, your dance with him got kinda heated."

"Something like that."

"What happened to him bringing a date? The guy seems to be a party of one tonight."

Last night, Evie had called John and confessed why she'd asked him to be her date. He was a great sport about it. So much so, he took it upon himself to layer on the affection when he felt Vincent was watching. But she, too, wondered what happened to Vincent's expected companion.

"I'm going to head home." She strode back into the fray of activity that was still going strong and continued out into the hallway. John kept an even stride beside her. "But first…" She jabbed a thumb toward the door to the ladies' room.

"I'll have my car brought around and meet you out front."

"Okay." She ducked inside and quickly relieved herself, then found her friends and said good night. On her exit, the side door to the ballroom opened. Vincent emerged. Both stared back at the other, unblinking, without words. Within that uncomfortable moment, they seemed to pick up at the same time the sound coming from the coat room across the corridor. An argument was taking place in hushed tones behind the closed door. A low-pitched wail rang out. A woman's cry?

In a flash, Vincent charged, bursting in. Evie followed. She froze, eyes stretched wide, and slapped a hand over her mouth to stifle her resound gasp. *Oh sweet jeez!* Struck stunned, she couldn't look away from the tangled limbs, mussed hair, and disheveled clothes. *Goodness!* The sound hadn't been one of distress but that of passion. She and Vincent had interrupted Georgina Balaska Shaw and her ex-husband Harold Shaw's intimate tryst.

"Pardon," Vincent said to the couple, who were quickly righting their clothing.

"Sorry." Evie stepped back as Vincent hurriedly closed the door. They looked at one another. Both cut small smirks that dissipated just as fast.

The irony rang about as loud as church bells.

Vincent's lips pursed, but Evie pivoted and beelined it for the exit, choosing not to stick around to hear whatever it was he was about to say, letting her pride carry her out. Yet, the entire ride home, throughout her hot shower, and now lying in bed, staring up at the ceiling skylight, she couldn't stifle her gluttony for punishment—what was it Vincent wanted to say to her?

VINCENT PULLED INTO his driveway where one side of the garage door was already wide open. Sasha's car was parked within. That was a surprise. He rolled into the center spot, entered the *unlocked* door to the mudroom of his home, and stopped short. Stacked boxes lined the wall, three large, bulging suitcases, small appliances spread about, and a library of college textbooks littered the floor. *Hurricane Sasha.* She wasn't due to clean out her dorm suite for another week.

He tossed his keys into the ceramic dish stationed on the side table on his way into the kitchen, prepared to face the aftermath of the storm's arrival. Aside from a couple of drinking glasses in the sink, the space was otherwise in order. That was a first. Whenever his sister stayed over, his home turned upside down.

Over in the living room, the meteorologist's weather forecast of the DMV was displayed in brilliant, seventy-five-inch HD and amplified out of the surround sound. Sasha lay stretched out on the couch in her baggy nightshirt and toe-socks. With her tan-brown face covered in a green gunk, she bobbed her head beneath noise-canceling headphones while scrolling through her social media, completely unaware of him standing short yards away at the kitchen island. He crossed to her and grabbed the remote, turning off the TV she obviously wasn't watching.

"Oh!" Her head snapped up, whipping upright. "Vincent, you scared the living crap out of me."

Remnants of popcorn kernels lay at the bottom of the glass bowl on the floor. "You're lucky it's me and not some serial nutjob. You left the garage door up and the side entry unlocked. Your stuff is cluttering up my floor."

"Oh. Right. I decided to move out of my suite early to avoid the rush next week. Maren was here helping me go over my guest list for the party. I told her to turn the lock on her way out." Smiling, she held out her phone, showing him a long list of names. "This party's gonna be lit."

"You should've made certain the door was locked."

"Peesh." She waved a dismissing hand. "No one's trying to come into this snooty neighborhood. Besides, it has twenty-four seven security patrol."

And it was a far cry from how he grew up. Sixteen years Sasha's senior, Vincent had moved their parents out of the three-bedroom apartment and into a modest, single-family home before his baby sister got to experience the full effect of what it meant to live working-class poor.

"How was the wedding?"

"Good." Evie had looked so damn beautiful tonight. He couldn't take his eyes off her and cursed himself for his weakness over the way she so easily stirred his senses.

Exhausted, he loosened his tie and took a seat on the opposite couch, practically melding into the thick comfort of the cushions.

He tried to think of a way to soften the bad news, but no reasonable explanation, except that he'd fucked up, came to mind. *Straight talk.*

"I won't be able to get the custom cake."

Her eyes stretched, then her astonished look rolled into visible disappointment.

"I didn't get the order in soon enough. They're booked. I screwed up; I know. I'm really sorry." He felt like shit.

"I knew this would happen if you waited too long. I said I could take care of it, but you insisted you'd do it. You know the owner of Chase Confections, Kennedi Chase. She just married your best friend. Doesn't that count for something? Maybe explain to her that you forgot to place the order."

It would be Kennedi's partner, Evie, he'd have to confront. The likelihood of her doing him a favor was slim to none. "How about I cover an all-expenses-paid trip of your choice for you and your friend, Maren? You've been saying for a long time that it's something you want to do after you graduate."

"I told you Maren, Telesha, and I are going to New Orleans this summer. That trip has been booked for months."

Had she? "I don't recall you saying that. Sorry."

"Yeah, you forgot. Big surprise. Why do I even bother telling you?" She snatched the hair band from the center table and gathered up her long braids with jerky movements, forming a thick topknot at her crown. "It's not like you listen to anything I say."

When she'd decided to come to D.C. for college, their parents had asked him to look after her. He'd been doing a mediocre job of it lately. "What if I got you a car?"

"I have a car."

"It has a lot of miles on it."

"Duh, it's a '69 Mustang convertible. But it runs great. You should know."

He did. With the custom upgrades he'd put into it, the car would outlive the sun. Still, he owed her a consolation for his fuck-up. "You've had it since high school. I thought you might like a new one." His cell phone rang, momentarily diverting his attention. As he pulled it from his pocket to check the display, he flashed a hand up to try to get her to stay put, but she grabbed her headphones and unfolded herself from the couch.

"No on getting me a new car, but thanks. I like my car. It's special to me," she muttered on her way upstairs.

Vincent felt worse than shit. Rarely did she ask him for anything. Though he paid for her schooling, she held a part-time job while carrying a full course load. Finished an entire year early and had carried a stellar GPA throughout. Yet he couldn't secure a simple goddamn custom cake order, something she'd asked for since her sophomore year. *Damn.*

He headed to his bedroom and peeled out of his suit, in need of a hot shower. As he removed his watch and placed it with his cell on the nightstand, Evie's business card lay face up. As if he needed that tug that never left his conscience. He sat on the edge of the bed, flipped the card over, and scooped it up along with his phone. The digital clock read 9:50. She'd left the reception tonight only a few minutes before he did. Maybe she was still with her date, extending their evening. As he tapped in her number, he took pleasure in possibly disrupting any horizontal play. By the fourth ring, he had to force himself to unclench his teeth, picturing the two together, and prepped himself to leave a message. He was struck into stunned silence when the sing-soft sound of her voice brushed his eardrum. "Evening. It's Vincent."

"I'm...I'm aware," she said through a heavy breath. "I recognized the number."

Her intermittent pants were irrefutable. *She and John... What in all the fuck...* Speculating that the two were together was one thing, but... Irritation, undercut by fierce jealousy, hit Vincent with a severe punch. "Sounds like I interrupted something. I'll let you get back to whatever you—"

"Jus-just a minute." A fumbling sound filled the line followed by a resounding *clunk.* "I'm back. I was on my elliptical."

"Elliptical? You're working out?"

"That's typically what it's used for."

A wave of tension left his shoulders. "Do you still medi-tate? You were also big into holistic treatment." His attempt to lighten the mood was met by a heavy exhalation.

"What is it you called for, Mr. Scott? I'd like to finish my workout to clear my head…cleanse my auric space and get to bed. I have work in the morning. You've made abundantly clear tonight your view of me, not that I wasn't already clued in."

"That's partially why I'm calling. I'd like to apologize. It was wrong of me to come at you the way that I did tonight."

"Tonight? Try whenever we're in the same space. You make it a point to act as though I don't exist. Oh, wait. That's pretty much what you said to me at your office—we don't have a history. On that note, good night—"

"Wait! Don't hang up." Her defensively cold reply was justified. He needed to turn things around if he was going to get his favor granted. "I shouldn't have said that."

Silence ticked for slow seconds. "Okay, and…?"

"And I'm sorry."

"You said it was *partially* the reason for your call." The softness in her voice returned.

"Right. Well, my sister, Sasha, just finished up at Ameri-can University. She's having a graduation party in a little more than three weeks. I meant to place an order for a custom cake as a gift, but I've been so busy, it slipped my mind."

"We have orders scheduled well into late August."

He didn't expect she'd have any sympathy strings for him to pull on. "Yes, Tabitha mentioned that. I just thought maybe—"

"You spoke with Tabitha? Did she tell you she's only working part-time during her pregnancy?"

"Yes." The line went silent for a moment once more.

"Kennedi will be away on her honeymoon for the next couple of weeks. So, you didn't really call to apologize. You had no other option."

"Yes… No…" *Shit.* "I had every intention to apologize to you tonight, but—"

"But I guess, as with not placing the custom cake order in a timely manner, it slipped your mind. Like I said, we're booked. Good night, Mr. Scott."

The line went dead.

Fuck.

Chapter Six

THE BLARE OF the alarm clock made Evie slap at the nightstand, knocking the annoyance to the floor. She buried her head beneath the pillow. Six thirty a.m. on a Sunday was the worst. Especially when sleep came in short clips. She'd tossed about all night. Vincent and his self-serving apology. She was done feeling guilty, tired of carrying the full weight of the blame.

Sleeping in wasn't an option, not with Kennedi away and Tabitha at half capacity. Aside from manning the store, Evie had taken up Tabitha's intern-training duties as well. She rolled out of bed and dragged herself to the bathroom.

The steam shower on high, she sat on the bench, eyes closed, head back against the tile, and let the heat warm her blood and awaken her muscles.

Large hands parted her knees to fit his wide shoulders. Determined fingers roamed over her hips and toyed with her breasts, bringing them to stiff achy peaks. Smooth lips followed the wet angle of her throat down and captured a nipple with his teeth, tugging, sucking. His head ducked lower still, kissing her middle as his calloused fingertips found and explored her clit before the eager sweep of his tongue took over. As his mouth worked her sex into a frenzy of need, her hands cupped the neat, short crop of his hair, holding him steady, right where—

Evie's head dipped forward, jolting her awake. She jumped up, breath sawing, blinking rapidly through the mist and peering at the fogged shower glass. *What in the…?* It was a dream, but more of a memory. A point in time from her past so vivid, every beat. The way the rough, worked surface of Vincent's hands gently touched her face as he took his time kissing her. How he cupped her breasts, caressing her nipples in teasingly slow swirls. The way the pad of his fingers lightly grazed up her thighs before sinking deep inside her. How their bodies melded as one… She shook her head. Vincent was her past. And the loss had been excruciating for her. An ache crawled into her throat, reminded of the pain that had torn her up inside, but she shoved it back and drew on her firm detachment. She turned on the ceiling spray, scrubbed with rough purpose, and got out.

No more steam showers.

A BRILLIANT KALEIDOSCOPE of sunrays cut through the glass storefront and followed Evie inside. Staff were setting tables and righting chairs after last night's floor buffing.

"Morning, everyone." She crossed to the counter where Amy and Tabitha's newest apprentice, Brielle, were sipping coffee and chatting while counting the register drawer for the day.

"Bri, give me thirty minutes to take care of a few items on my desk, then we'll get started on creating the locomotive for the Jenkins's order."

"I can't wait!" An eager smile spread across Brielle's cute, pink face.

Evie headed to her office and turned on the computer. About fifteen minutes into answering emails, a knock came at the door before it opened. She glanced up. Brielle poked her head inside. "Bri, I'll be done here soon."

"No, you have a visitor. It's…your husband."

Before Evie's brain could catch up, tanned fingers gripped the edge of the door above Brielle's petite frame and widened the opening.

"Good morning." Patrick stepped into the office. "Thought I'd come visit my wife on this lovely Sunday morning. Maybe get a tour of the place."

She took note of Brielle's quizzical look. No wedding ring, no loving photos adorning the office—nothing gave evidence to his claim. Few knew about Evie's pain-in-the-ass husband. Well, Amy knew tidbits—she'd been working at the bakery for a while—and would've had Patrick remain out front. Evie mostly kept her personal life personal. She surely didn't bring her drama to work.

"Where's Amy?" she asked Brielle and came to her feet, circling from behind the desk.

"She went to make a drop box deposit."

"Thanks, Bri. I'll come find you in a bit." Evie closed the door and swung around to see Patrick standing there with a jolly smile on his face. She funneled all the will within not to smack it off. "What the hell is wrong with you, coming here? This is my place of business."

"Like I said, I wanted to visit my wife and perhaps get a

look at the place. Where's the harm in that? I guess my invite to the grand opening got lost in the mail."

Evie bit the inside of her jaw to hold on to her patience. "Why in hell would I invite you? We're in the middle of a divorce."

He sat on the edge of the desk, fiddling with the papers. "But we don't have to be."

She snatched her bank ledger from his prying gaze and stuck it into the drawer. "You've never cared before about my work, even referred to it as a hobby. Not once did you step foot in the old store. Now, suddenly, you want a tour?"

"I was afraid the roof might collapse on my head." He laughed low. "I'm kidding. Don't look so serious." He moved to the bookshelves, took down one of the cake design binders, thumbed the pages, and delivered a glance over his shoulder as he set it back in place, carefully checking that all the spines were neatly aligned. Soon, soon, soon, she'd be free from his control even in her own domain. "Ann, you know you never had to work. I have the means and took care of you. Quite frankly, you've never wanted for anything. I thought this bakery partnership with your friends was you finding something to do with your time."

The care he dished out came at a price she no longer wanted to pay. "My work isn't a hobby, and I have a lot of it to do today, so you need to go."

He threw his hands up with an agitated pace in a tight circle, then faced her. "I can't come to your store. I can't go to the house where I'm still paying the damn mortgage. You don't respond to texts or return my calls." He sighed long, combing fingers on both hands through his salon-cut blond hair, then moved to her, his gaze roaming, settling on her face in that measuring way of his. More characteristics that fell within the OCPD spectrum. Clinical studies showed the best way to avoid aggravating heightened compulsions was to remain calm.

His hand came up toward her cheek, but Evie stepped back. "Wearing your hair tied back is your thing now, I see. What else have you changed…aside from choosing to end our life together?" Another sigh. "Stop this foolishness, Ann. It's gone on long enough."

His tone was soft, but there was a clear command she was expected to obey. And he hated when she wore a ponytail, saying that the style was for little girls, not women.

The sooner she played nice, the sooner he'd leave. "You want a tour? Fine, let's go." She pulled open the door and marched out into the hall. He remained in the office, staring back at her, his cool blue eyes returning to amused curiosity. "Well? There really isn't much to see."

"Lead the way."

They went into the kitchen. Carlos had the place busy prepping. Over in the custom cake design room, Brielle was there getting things set up to work on the locomotive design but darted from the room when they entered. She'd put out the tools and the sketches Evie had drawn with scale markings for the train, to use as a guide.

Patrick picked up the paper. "You're making this?"

She cut a narrowed look at him. He sounded surprised. "It's what I do here, and I really need to get to it." A glance at her watch showed they were due to open in about thirty minutes. She moved to the door. "Patrick, out." He followed her to the storefront. Amy was back behind the counter. Her brow rose as Evie passed by.

Patrick stopped and stuck out his hand, all smiles. "Hi, we haven't met. You weren't here when I said my hellos to everyone. I'm Patrick Powell."

"Hi, I'm Amy."

"Nice to meet you, Amy. What's your role here?"

"I'm—"

"Patrick?" Evie ground down tight on her molars, trying her damnedest not to show her searing emotions in front of the staff. "Amy's our storefront supervisor. She has work to do… Everyone has work to do." He followed Evie toward the exit.

"Sweetheart, say you'll stop this nonsense about a divorce."

The problem with high ceilings and a large, practically empty space was that voices carried, damn near echoing. Evie froze at the door, her hand squeezing the push bar. She turned and stared up at his smirking face. Then saw that her entire staff—gaping back at her—looked just as shockingly stiff. She gnashed her teeth to keep it together and walked outside, moving several paces away from the entrance, then whirled around, all of her patience gone. "Don't come back here. Ever. You didn't give a damn about what I do here when we were together. I don't need you to pretend to care now."

"How was I to know you were serious when you couldn't even settle on an area of focus? You have three degrees, two of which are masters in fields that would've brought you in far better financial position than becoming a baker with your friends whose business was about to tank."

She threw her arms out wide and twirled toward the new red-brick storefront. "As you can see, we're doing just fine."

"I see." He nodded. "I'm only asking that you give us another chance."

She took in a breath and let it go slowly. "Patrick, sometimes two people aren't a good fit. And I'm at a different place in my life. Why can't you just accept that?"

"The guy you were with at the wedding, is he a good fit?" That flicker of a simmering temper flashed in his blue eyes.

"How do you…? Are you…you're stalking me?" She breathed deep, drained by his drama. "I'm not doing this again with you. Who I see and what I do is none of your business." She pivoted, walking back toward the store, but he caught her wrist and jerked hard enough that she spun off-balance, stumbling over her own feet. "What the hell? Let go of me."

"You're my goddamn wife," he gritted out. "It's sure as hell my business." His jaw formed into rigid angles as he yanked her closer. "Are you fucking him in my house, our bed?"

Before she could think, her palm met his cheek hard enough his head swung sideways, but his hand clutching her wrist only tightened, crushing it. She bit back a whimper, refusing to acknowledge the pain shooting up her arm. "This right here is why we're getting a divorce—your narcissistic need to control. Now, let go before I—"

"You heard the lady."

Evie's head whipped around to see Vincent crossing in

determined, long-legged strides. He came to stand beside her, shifting just enough into Patrick's space to be threatening.

"She told you to let her go."

Patrick's brow furrowed tight. "I'm having a discussion with my wife. How about you mind your own damn business."

Vincent took a step forward. "I suggest you leave while you still can on your own."

His voice was calm—calm before the storm—and the grin he wore chilled her to the marrow. Twelve years, yet she still knew what Vincent's look meant. She wrenched free of Patrick's hold in the hope of saving him from himself as she gave a glance about at the slowly increasing foot traffic waking up the Wharf. "Just go, Patrick."

Patrick eyed Vincent up and down. "Ann, who's this clown?"

"Clown?" Vincent chuckled deep in his throat. "I see you're that guy. Chest poking out, talking tough. You'll assault a woman, but let's see how far you get if you try that shit with me."

Patrick stepped in close, the men practically nose to nose. He flashed his antagonizing glare from Vincent to Evie then back to Vincent. "So, you're the one screwing my wife."

What happened next was a blur. Patrick made an about-face with what appeared to be the smart choice to leave. But he pivoted back and swung on Vincent. As if anticipating it, Vincent's head darted with perfect counter trajectory, caught Patrick's arm, spun him, and pinned the limb in a terrible bend at the man's back. The right shoulder socket looked ready to snap. The groan of violent pain was evident in the rapid, red wash of Patrick's face.

"No more showing up here or at her home without an invite. Now find your damn vehicle and get gone," Vincent snarled, dropping Patrick straight down to his knees.

"You're going to pay for this," Patrick hissed, struggling to his feet. "Ann, this is on you. You and him… Your behavior, now it all makes sense," he growled, and stumbled to his Porsche illegally taking up Evie's reserved parking spot in front of the store. "You want a divorce? You'll get it. Starting with me getting my cut of this here store of yours. Oh, and tell your dad that I quit," he yelled on a screeching drive away as several patrons who'd watched the scene play out headed into the bakery.

Ugh.

Humiliated, Evie could hardly look Vincent in the eye, not wanting to witness his judgment or his pity. She tried to skirt past him, but he touched her wrist lightly. Gentle fingers brushed over her bruised flesh, examining the welts and scrapes of broken skin.

"You need to clean this so it doesn't get infected." His eyes held hers, and she didn't move away as tender fingers tucked those loose locks behind her ear. He gently took hold of her other arm, turning it at all angles, his attention roaming upward, giving her extremities a long study. His eyes hardened. "Has he done this before?"

Evie shook her head, but it only made his thick brows knit tighter. "He says things that are…" She wasn't about to get into this with her ex-boyfriend. "He hasn't."

"What an asshole. And why the hell does he call you by

your middle name? What did you ever see in that fool?"

She stalked off, so damn tired of it all. "I don't have the energy to talk about Patrick right now. He drains me." She was vividly aware of her life mistakes and didn't need to hear them aloud.

"Hold up. Evie, wait." He jogged after her and blocked the entrance. "Sorry you have to deal with that."

"Why are you even here?"

"I was hoping to work out something with you on making a cake. After what I saw here, I'm thinking we can help each other. I can represent you in your divorce, and you can create a graduation cake for my sister. Have you hired an attorney yet?"

"No, and no to you representing me. You're my ex. Oh, wait. That's right, we don't have history." She tried to reach around his big body for the door handle, but he pressed back against it. "Vincent, move."

"Evie—"

"What happened to calling me Mrs. Powell?" She glared up into his goddamn handsome face. Stirringly gorgeous from the depths of his rich-brown eyes filled with intensity and integrity, to the tender yet deeply soulful sound of his voice. "I really need you to move. I have work to do."

"*Evie*," he stressed her name softly. "Let me take away this burden for you. I've handled numerous cases like yours. I love to tackle individuals like Patrick. And judging by what I witnessed today, he's going to try to make you suffer."

"He already has," she muttered. But she kept her emotions tightly sealed to her chest, refusing to let the tears stinging the backs of her eyes break free.

"I'll deal with his attorney and keep you shielded from it all until it's time to sign the papers. As a matter of fact, first order of business will be to get a restraining order that'll prevent him from coming within five hundred damn feet of you," he ground out.

It was music to her ears. Her ex-boyfriend, who stirred a strange quiver in her belly at the mere sight of him and who she wasn't on the best of terms with, would represent her in divorcing her husband. *What a conundrum.* Nevertheless, she shook her head. "No."

"May I ask why you haven't gotten a restraining order? I can see the stress Patrick puts on you."

"It would only exacerbate his condition; one he pretends doesn't exist."

"Condition?"

"Obsessive-compulsive personality disorder. Patrick would see the restraining order as an affront, thereby igniting an anxiety to convince the person who'd accused him—me—that he was wrongly judged. Add to that his narcissism, and it makes for an explosive cocktail. He's pretty much stayed away. It wasn't until I fired my attorney that he started coming around. He thought…thinks I've decided not to pursue a divorce."

"Considering you're openly dating, I'd guess you are moving ahead with it." The hard angle of Vincent's jaw ticked as he held her gaze, unblinking.

She didn't correct him. John Seils had been the first man she'd stepped out with since her separation a little over a year ago. "I have a lot to do today."

He moved away from the door.

She entered the store but stood at the glass and watched him as he moved with a relaxed, even gait, his medium-blue denims hugging his long legs and nice ass. *What a perfect ass.* She used to enjoy watching him. The way his muscles flexed beneath his glistening brown skin. The well-defined sculpt of his shirtless back. She'd sit for hours at the garage while he worked, sweat beading his strong neck and shoulders. That small storage room in the back of Joe's shop became their spot when everyone was out on roadside calls. He'd lift her dress, slip her panties down her legs with unhurried hands on his way down to his knees. Take his time pleasuring her with his soft lips and warm tongue before sliding his cock into the heat of her, working her body to the brink of madness.

"Evie?"

Startled, she twirled to Amy standing behind her. "Hey." With her breath a tad labored, Evie gave herself a hard mental slap. She hadn't had sex in so long; here she was groping the man with her eyes.

"Is everything all right?" Amy peered out the window, then turned back. "I had a talk with Bri. She'll know next time not to let anyone in the back without asking me first."

"Hope you weren't too hard on her. Patrick told her he was my husband. She didn't know he was also a dick." Evie grinned and succeeded in softening the scowl on the young woman's face. "I should get to work...lots to do today." On a sigh, she trotted off toward the rear and spent a good bit of the day training Bri. The apprentice was a quick learner. They managed to get the train's tracks completed. While the gum paste set, Evie tackled paperwork, which was usually Kennedi's responsibility. She was looking forward to things getting back to normal. That said, remaining busy, the hours flew by.

Later lying in bed, her mom on speakerphone, she searched the internet for a reputable divorce attorney. She also kept a glance on the flat screen across the room.

"Ooh, look, Shemar's shirtless again. He's hot," her mom crooned.

"Ew, Mom," She teased. It was her mom's turn to pick which show to binge-watch this month. Like the *S.W.A.T.* star—hot, brainy, black guy—her mom had a type. Well, her dad didn't fit the black part. He had a more Pierce Brosnan look about him—tall, broad physique, strong square jaw, and a full head of dark hair with only sprinkled amounts of gray at the temples. Retired army, his regimented five a.m. military workout was engrained and kept him in good shape. Her parents had the kind of bond Evie hoped to find someday.

"What's wrong with me saying he's hot? He's aged very well."

"Nothing's wrong with it." She grabbed her wineglass from the nightstand and took a sip. "Am I going to have to hear you drool every time Shemar's swoony, sexy face and naked chest appear on screen?" They both laughed. "I need to find myself a Shemar Moore." Evie chortled, only half joking.

"Sweetheart, have you found an attorney? I'm sorry you're having to go through this with Patrick. I wish there was more I could do. I would've loved to see things work out for you two. But always know I'm in your corner."

The comforting support enveloped her like the warmth

of a cozy sweater and couldn't have come at a better time, quieting the anxiety within. Evie saw it as an opening and told her Mom what took place with Patrick at the store but didn't mention Vincent. Not sure why other than back in the day when they'd dated, her mom never really took to him.

"My goodness! Why didn't you tell me he'd been behaving this way?"

"You kept pushing for us to stay together. I know you like him, and you're friends with his mother. I guess I thought you'd be disappointed in me."

"Disappointed in you? Never! Now you listen. Get yourself a good lawyer and rid yourself of that man, you understand?"

"I'm trying. Has Patrick told Dad he quit?"

"You know your father's close-lipped about his work. It's the military in him. If Patrick quit, good riddance. Don't you worry about that. You just concentrate on finding a lawyer."

Had she made the right call in not hiring Vincent? Frankly, despite everything going on in her life, Vincent had managed to crowd her thoughts most of all. Regret of what could have been between them haunted her. She used to love to hear him talk about cars, the way his eyes sparkled when an old model rolled into the garage for him to tackle. And how excited he became when she'd ask the simplest question about an engine part.

The strong attraction she admittedly still had for Vincent also taunted her.

Did he have a girlfriend? An irrational irritation stirred.

She'd charted every inch of smooth skin over hard muscle that rippled across his body. Who got the pleasure of scaling that beautifully chiseled terrain now?

Her cell phone chimed a text. Anticipating her girlfriends' nightly check in, she took another good gulp from her glass, then set it on the nightstand. Before she could type a quick reply, her phone rang. *Vincent.* She swallowed so hard the dry cabernet slid down her throat like molten lava. "Mom, I have a call coming in. I'll talk to you tomorrow."

"Try to finish this episode so we don't fall behind. Good night, sweetheart."

"Okay. Good night." On a bracing breath, she sat up and opened the line. "Vincent."

"Good evening, Evie."

The deep, rich rumble of his voice was like warm fingers caressing along the nape of her neck. Her entire body suddenly tingled. She grabbed her glass and sucked down every drop.

"Evie?"

"Um-hum."

"Given what happened today with Patrick, I thought I'd check on you. Are you home?"

"I'm in bed. How about you? Are you in bed, Vinny?" She slapped a hand over her mouth. *Why did I say that? And why the hell am I talking all low and husky?*

"Vinny?" He cleared his throat on a soft chuckle. "It's been a long time since I've heard that."

"I-I mean, Vincent." *Shit.* He hated the nickname, but she used to call him that in private when…when their hands and mouths touched and tasted, groped and licked.

Evie, stop!

"Yes, I'm in bed getting work done before I turn in. I wanted to send you some info I pulled together."

"What is it?"

"I call it my war sheet—notes I typically write down on the attorney I'm going up against. In this instance, it's a few bullet points on Patrick's legal counsel—his strengths, weaknesses, case history, his wins and losses. The guy plays dirty. He'll take everything he can get for his client down to the floorboards."

"Oh. Okay." She didn't know what to say. The act was so like him.

"It should be in your inbox now. Anyway, just thought it might help your attorney prepare."

She quickly pulled up her email and opened the document. A few notes? There were two full pages of information. Even lines about Patrick's actions today at the bakery. Appreciation and most of all, a strong sense of longing—the emotions washed over her, roiling like turbulent waves. She used to say he had the heart of a tiger and the soul of an angel. "Thank you."

"Well, I'll let you go. Have a good night, Evie."

"You, too. Good night."

But she wasn't ready to hang up.

Chapter Seven

V INCENT GAVE A wide yawn just as the elevator doors parted on the main level of his law practice. Last night may have resulted in two, maybe three at most, consecutive hours of sleep.

The time he'd spent putting together the war sheet for Evie set him back on prepping his court deposition. But it was only partly why exhaustion had a hold on him this morning. Every time he closed his eyes her face appeared. The soft cadence of her voice lingered in his head like a siren song, playing long after their call ended. By the time night had crept into dawn, he'd stopped fighting with himself, gave in to the heady trance of attraction he still had for her, and succumbed to his torturous baser desires. *Is it wrong to beat off to the image of your married ex-girlfriend who you still have a thing for?*

The question was about as fucked-up as they came.

"Vincent, good morning." Jasmine jumped to her feet. Her heels tapped the tile as she hurried from behind the receptionist desk with a wad of messages for him in her outstretched hand.

He'd long ago given up telling her it wasn't necessary to greet him like a loyal subject. He didn't hand out brownie points. Her dedicated work ethic was enough. "I have to prepare for court." On his way toward the stairs, he held up the slips of paper while fighting back another yawn. "Is there anything in here that can't wait until I return this afternoon?" Law clerks greeted him with eager smiles from behind their file-stack desks, and junior associates on phone calls within glass-front offices delivered nods as he strode past. Some stood, making certain to be seen. He'd been where they were, worn their shoes, and appreciated their dedication. Most of all, billable hours were a good thing.

Jasmine kept a quick patter of feet behind him. "No, but there's someone here to see you."

"I don't have any appointments this morning." He glanced back at her as he moved. "And we don't take walk-ins. You know that."

"I do. I was about to tell Mrs. Powell I'd have to check your schedule but—"

He swiveled suddenly, and she nearly ran into him. "Did you say Mrs. Powell?"

"Yes. I was going to schedule a time for her to return, but—"

"But I stopped her."

Vincent turned back around. Across the open-space concept of thick leather chairs and couches, the youngest of his senior partners stood within the doorframe of her office. Shimmers of sunlight bathed the east row of suites, obscuring her face within the glare as she shrugged into her navy suit jacket. Sloane Ellis freed her long, dark tresses trapped at the collar before clasping hold of the black leather briefcase stationed by her stilettos and came forward. Fitted skirt and a neatly tucked, white silk blouse with the top two buttons free to show just enough smooth brown skin, she moved with a confident sway. And why wouldn't she? Top of her class at Yale. Her number of case wins matched his—one loss to her record. It was why he'd selected her as a partner, that and the fact she was prepared to put up the required capital to join on the spot.

"Morning, Sloane." He glanced at his watch. "Aren't you due in court?"

"As are you. I'm headed there now. I thought we'd ride over together, but you have a visitor. I know you removed the Powell case from the roster, but Mrs. Powell was Rosati's client. Obviously, she's here for a reason. I figured you'd want to know what that might be. I had her wait in your office." She strode toward the stairs. "See you over at District."

Vincent headed to his corner office. The largest of the suites, the space didn't get the terrific wake-me-up shards of sunbeams, but there was that direct line of sight to the Washington Monument. If ever he doubted how far he'd come, all he had to do was look out his window.

He paused a moment at the door to take in the sight of Evie standing before the carousel assortment of K-Cups. The off-the-shoulder coral dress accentuated the warm fair-brown coloring of her delicate skin and hugged her soft curves, likely tailor-cut just for her. A tease of athletic thighs, sleek knees, and trim calves was getting a rise out of him. Shit, it had been a while since he'd gotten laid, which was partially the reason for the spike in desire. But the renewed fever level of attraction was much more than that. It was simply her.

French vanilla. Wait for it... He smirked when she plucked her favorite blend from among the many pods of dark roasted. As she prepared the cup, her head turned toward him entering. A smile touched her blush lips. Damn, she was beautiful and sexy without even trying.

Vincent put on his game face to curtail the sudden stab of lust. "This is a surprise. Good morning." He moved past her, circling behind his desk, and set his briefcase on it but didn't sit, since she remained standing.

"Good morning, Vincent. I hope you don't mind. I helped myself." She grabbed an empty mug and snagged a pod. "Black, no sugar?"

"Yes."

As a steady stream of rich chicory flowed, she grabbed her coffee and turned to him. Her gaze held his as she lightly blew on her drink, wafting the steam. "I know I don't have an appointment, so I'll get right to it. I want you to represent me in my divorce. In return, I'll create your sister's graduation cake." She scooped the newly brewed cup, came to the front of the desk, and handed it over.

On impulse, he gently took her wrist and examined the purpling bruise where her ex had left his mark. Vincent ran his thumb lightly over the area. He should have snapped that fucker's bones in two. "Does it hurt?"

"I'm fine. Here."

He took the cup but didn't let go of his grasp on her until she tugged lightly. "You said our past involvement would be an issue. What changed?"

"Well, let's face it. I know where you stand in that department."

"Do you now?" Because he sure as hell was struggling with the answer. Had he not glanced up from his coffee, which helped to awaken his senses from the first sip, he would've missed the flash of something that surfaced in her expression and disappeared just as fast.

"Look—" she sat her cup down next to his and rounded the desk, coming to stand before him "—it's difficult to find a good attorney in this city who's accepting new clients, and one I trust will ensure Patrick and his legal goons don't try to strong-arm me." Slender fingers scrubbed across her forehead as she heaved a sigh. "I just want this over with. He won't let me be."

Without thinking, instinctively, he palmed her waist and drew her protectively to his chest, holding her close, wanting to take away her look of dismay.

Her head came up; her arms circling around his shoulders loosened. As if realizing her position, she lightly pushed him away, spine straightening, that familiar bravado turned on strong. "Do we have a deal? It's the very same arrangement you offered me not twenty-four hours ago." She stuck out her hand.

Warm. Soft. Reminiscent of the rest of her. He attempted to match the all-business civility in her voice. "We have a deal." His cell phone buzzed. "My driver's downstairs. I'm late for court." Neither moved, their gazes holding steady. In that moment, he felt spellbound by her. Her fragrance held him captive like a seductively cunning temptress's weapon. It would explain why all lucidity seemed to disappear whenever her scent wafted his nose.

She slipped her hands free from his, breaking the trance.

"I guess you should get going."

Vincent blinked. "Right." He grabbed his briefcase and stuffed the folders he came for into it. She retrieved her purse from the chair in front of the desk. "We'll need to schedule a time to meet to go over the particulars of your case. How about Friday here at one?" he said on their way out and down the stairs.

"Okay."

On the elevator, he glanced over when she brought out her phone and pulled up Uber. "Where are you headed? My driver can take you wherever you need to go."

"You don't have to do that."

"I know I don't have to. Now where?"

"Chase Confections. But it'll put you out of your way."

The elevator doors slid open. They crossed the lobby and exited the building in step together. His driver held the rear door open at the curb. "Morning, Jim. I got it." Vincent followed her inside and ignored the quizzical look she delivered him when he chose to sit across from her. He needed a little distance. "About the cake. Sasha would like it with her wearing her cap and gown."

"I remember Sasha. She was a cute little girl. I can't believe she's graduating college."

"She's far from little." Vincent pulled out his cell and showed her a picture. "She's about as tall as I am."

Evie smiled. "She's beautiful. Remember that time you had to watch her over a weekend while your parents were away? She'd get out of her bed and come jump on the couch, squirming her way between us beneath the blanket. You'd return her to her room, and she'd come right back. Over and over. Then you bribed her to stay put with all the ice cream and cookies she wanted." Evie laughed softly. "She fell asleep in a sugar coma."

Vincent chuckled. "Yeah, just long enough for you and me to…" It had been a shared night of hot, urgent intimacy. Longing for her struck so hard and swift, he could barely withstand the pressure building in his chest. He cleared his throat, pushing away the memory, and tried for casualness amid the awkwardness. "For the cake, what do you need from me?"

"I'll start with a picture of her."

She spoke in a low, shaky tone, her eyes averted, her slender fingers fiddling with the hem of her dress. He could feel the tension, sensed the caution she kept erected. He mirrored those emotions and didn't know how to get past his own steel barrier.

He made a few taps on his phone. "Sent."

The car slowed and their heads turned toward the window as the driver came to a stop in front of the District Courthouse. The door opened. Jim stood at attention. Vincent slid over and offered up a small smile. "I would've done the gentlemanly thing and seen you to your store, but as I said, I'm late. Jim will get you there. Take care, Evie."

"You, too."

EVIE LOOKED ON as Vincent exchanged a few words with Jim, some that included seeing her to her destination. He glanced back at her through the lightly tinted window, his attorney attitude fully in place before he jetted up the courthouse steps.

The second the car started moving, she eased her head back against the seat and released a long, uneven breath, yearning for what she knew was long out of her reach. Yet the calmingly deep cadence of his voice, his attentiveness, and even the mere whiff of his cologne, tossed her back in time where she'd felt loved and protected with an all-consuming trust and devotion. But she didn't fool herself. When he'd touched her, held her within his comforting warmth, it was instinct that drove his need to soothe her distress—it had always been his nature, nothing more.

She secretly hung on to those memory threads. Her heart refused to let them die. Knowing the feelings were one-sided kept her from any foolish illusions.

Chapter Eight

"I DON'T THINK hiring your ex is a good idea. It's D.C. There have to be a ton of attorneys out there."

As Evie hummed in tempo to the music, she kept her rolling pin in motion, thinning out the cherry-red fondant to the proper thickness for the caboose. She looked at Tabitha across the prep table, reading objection aplenty in her direct stare. They'd been discussing and disagreeing on Evie's choice of legal counsel all evening.

"Tab, Vincent has a law degree from Georgetown. His clients are among those on the Hill, and his firm is one of the best in the area." Her hand slipped, breaking a corner off the train track. "Shit."

"Here. Let me." Tabitha rounded the table and got to work with the sugar paste, repairing the damage, then set the yard-long track of chocolate gum paste on its wooden base.

Evie shifted out of the way. She knew Tabitha was happy to be back at the store, albeit part-time. She'd pretty much taken over the project—not that Evie minded. She welcomed the help.

"Tab, I'm just trying to get things with Patrick over and done. He's making it difficult, as you well know. Vincent can take care of this for me."

"I'm not questioning his level of expertise," she said while together, they carefully situated each railcar in place. "My concern is about you making more out of it than him performing a professional service to a client." She straightened, rolling her shoulders, a hand palming her hip. "Girlfriend, let's keep it one hundred—I don't think you're over him."

A flutter of anxiousness flooded Evie's chest. "What are you talking about?"

"Case in point: you had my brother, John, pretend to be your boyfriend at Kennedi's wedding on the mere speculation that Vincent was bringing a date." Tabitha's lips quirked a little. "If that doesn't say you're in your feelings about him, I don't know what will."

Evie drew back at her friend's tried-and-true directness. "Okay, I'll admit the fake boyfriend thing was immature of me. But what Vincent and I had is in the past. I hired him to settle my divorce. In return, I've agreed to create a cake for his sister. It's strictly business between us. What? Why are you looking at me like that?"

Tabitha's scrutiny didn't waver.

Evie was about to offer a second dose of reassurance when Tabitha's cell phone rang, saving the need to bolster another feigned truth.

"It's Dom." Tabitha opened the line. "Hey, babe... Yes, I'm fine... How can you miss me? You popped in here for lunch." Her voice was soft, low...loving. On a chortle, she smiled, her cheeks coloring. With a shy glance at Evie, she stepped away to chat with her hubby.

Evie returned to her project, letting the overwhelming

fact of what she'd tried to convince herself sink in: Vincent was performing a job she'd hired him to do. Nothing more. No renewed feelings. No forgiveness for the past.

Her phone rang that time. She gave it a look and cringed. *Patrick.* When the ringing stopped, a voicemail notification popped up. *Not happening.*

Tabitha disconnected and turned back. "I better head home before Dom sends out the entire D.C. rescue unit for me. Until this baby comes, he's going to stay on edge."

"I'm sure." Evie glanced up at the clock over the door. "I didn't realize the time." It was crawling close to seven p.m. Tabitha had been in since noon, well past her doctor-recommended work hours.

Amy poked her head into the room. "Evie, there's a man out front asking to see you. He said his name's Vincent Scott." Amy's eyes rolled upward. "And oh my God, talk about hot! Face and body. My goodness, I'm telling you, he's got it all!"

It took a stomach-clenching second for Evie to speak. "Uh, you can send him back here. He's a friend. We'll be creating a cake for him." She felt a need to explain why she was breaking a store rule.

After Amy retreated, Evie turned to Tabitha. "I know what you're going to say."

Tabitha brought up a hand. "No judgment here. I'm only looking out for you. Sweetie, I don't want you to get hurt."

"I know, but it's not like that. It's a business arrangement." Evie smiled as she cemented the words firmly in her head.

A short moment later, Vincent's big, tall, bronze body filled the doorframe. Tailored designer suits or the simple Bob Marley T-shirt and nicely fitting denims that he now wore? She couldn't decide which look was hotter on him. Thick, naturally defined eyebrows that sloped downward gave him a smoldering look. Lips full and ripe. Bulging chest and biceps. A tight abdomen that said workouts were a regularly scheduled program. No one feature made him handsome, though the piercing intensity of his dark brown eyes took a solid lead.

"Good evening, ladies." He looked between them. "Didn't mean to interrupt. I was in the area." He directed his comment at Evie. "Thought I'd see if you were still in. I know we're scheduled to meet Friday, but there are a few items I wanted to go over with you before then."

"I better get home." Tabitha removed her apron and hugged Evie. "Be careful," she whispered at her ear then started toward the door. "Good seeing you, Vincent. Evie, don't forget, we're still on a week from Friday night. Kennedi will be back. Hope she remembers it's her turn to cook."

Evie looked forward to their once-a-month ladies' night in, with wine, food, and guy talk. They hadn't missed a meetup in nearly six years. Though now that her friends had spouses, their chats about men tended to steer toward how blissfully happy the two ladies were in their relationships. Evie felt more of a fifth, very wobbly wheel.

Vincent came forward and hunched, getting a look at the train design. "Wow!" His eyes went wide. "There are people inside the trolley." He glanced back at her. "This is really cool! Is it entirely edible? How did you make the window glass?"

"It's actually quite simple—boil sugar and water, then let it harden into a thin sheet. Being careful not to splinter it is the hardest part. Everything but the wooden base the cake is sitting on can be ingested."

He came out of his bend and eyed all the pictures covering the walls, of the many cake creations Evie, Tabitha, and Kennedi, and even those the founder of Chase Confections—Kennedi's late mother—had made over the years. "No wonder Sasha is hell-bent on having her cake done here. I knew you were talented, but all of this—" he gestured at the photos and over at the current project in the making "—it's amazing what you do." An awed look filled his eyes, and a smile emphasized his strong features. "Thanks again for agreeing to do it."

Evie ate up his praise and soaked up his admiration, but kept her feelings guarded from his gaze. "It's a business arrangement. A favor for a favor, right?"

"Right. Speaking of. I—" His phone rang, and he checked the display. "Excuse me; I need to take this." He stepped away. "Yes, my bad. Sorry about that. I meant to call. Something came up tonight." His voiced dropped. "That should work."

There was a distinct woman's voice. Evie tried to concentrate on cutting perfect circles for her wheels from the evenly rolled sheet of black fondant but...was it his girlfriend?

He made a soft laugh, followed by another. "Lunch tomorrow? I can work with that."

He's seeing someone. Her breath came out like a slow, silent, deflating balloon. *Of course, he would be. Look at him.*

He disconnected and returned to her at the prep table, his expression set into that neutrally cool mask.

"As I was about to say, I filed the restraining order today. Patrick's attorney likely received the notice this evening. No doubt he'll be communicating with his client. I'm guessing Patrick won't be happy about it. It's another reason I stopped by. I'll hang around to take you home." He pulled up a metal stool and half sat with a relaxed lean against the table, looking as though the matter was set and settled.

Not.

She returned to carving out her wheels. "Vincent, I—"

"Don't." He shook his head. "I know you're going to say no."

Her eyes flashed to his. "I don't need you to babysit me." She sighed. If only she could turn off her feelings about him. "I need to finish this tonight for pickup tomorrow. Working your sister's cake into the schedule means I can't waste a minute. There's another order I have to sketch before I can even start to design Sasha's cake. I don't know how late I'll be tonight, so you can go." He stared at her, eyes roaming, studying her face. "What are you looking at?" She bristled.

He shrugged a bulky shoulder. "Just admiring your freckles. Sixteen was the number long ago." His tone deep, pleasant, playful even, he came out of his leisurely slouch, stretching, rolling corded muscle. "Your glasses prevent me from getting an accurate count. You look adorable in them, by the way."

"You can save the buttering up." His words confused her. "I've already said I'd make your cake."

His brow lowered, puzzlement registering. "Sorry. I didn't mean anything by it. Old habit, I guess." The heavy silence that followed clouded the mood and reestablished their boundaries. "I'm going to go out front and grab a table, answer a few emails. When you're ready to leave, we'll leave."

As he headed toward the door, Evie turned up her music and let it help drive all her energy into her work. She cut, carved, and shaped, exacting corners. Piece after piece of sugary fondant got a touch of embellishment. When she looked up from her now finished creation, a good two hours had flown by.

After placing the cake into the walk-in freezer, she started the rough draft for the next design of a horse carrousel, straightened up, handled a few managerial matters with her two staff supervisors, Carlos and Amy, then made her way out front. She slowed her stride. Vincent was just where he said he'd be—seated in one of the leather chairs, his eyes leveled upward on the wall-mounted TV screen that blared ESPN. Amy must have set the channel for him. They typically ran foodie shows.

His attention shifted and landed on her. With that gorgeous face, strong physique, and shoot-from-the-hip attitude without being a hard-ass, no doubt he could charm anyone into doing just about whatever he wanted. She knew that about him. It was likely one of the reasons he was such a damn good attorney. And once upon a time, the best lover she'd ever had. Evie blinked.

Don't go there!

"Ready?" He unfolded his big body and came to his feet.

She shoved her misguided feelings back, along with the

hard punch of lust, and continued to the exit. He followed but then hurried ahead and caught the door, opening it for her.

"Did you finish the train?" he asked as she moved past him.

"Yes." Again, he jogged ahead and pulled opened the passenger door of a sleek, gray Tesla Roadster parked along the curb a short walk down the block.

She sank into the black, sporty leather seat as Vincent rounded the front of the car and slid in behind the wheel. "Remember that old '69 Camaro you bought off that guy for a thousand bucks?" She laughed. "You said it was a steal."

His gaze met hers, a small quirk twisting his mouth as he started the car. "It was a steal."

"It was rusted out and didn't have a back seat." She snorted. "The steering wheel fell clean off."

"Sure did." He laughed.

"Thank goodness we were about a block from home." They laughed together. The memory brought about warm feelings of a time once cherished. "What did you say to me?" She dropped some baritone into her voice to mimic his. "Evie, a solid block engine like this, you have to look beyond the rust. It's..."

"A diamond in the rough," they said in concert, sharing smirks.

"Actually, I said, 'Evie, my sweet...' You felt I'd wasted my money and made a point to say how irresponsible a purchase it'd been."

The glint in his eyes cooled, and the utter indignant visage that surfaced and closed off completely, said the walk down memory lane had come to an end. "My address—" she began.

"I got it from your file." He drove off, cutting into the slow-moving traffic.

As they inched along, headlights to taillights, he looked from her to the passenger window. Couples and small groups cut around cars, moving to and from the many nighttime activities happening on the Wharf's boardwalk.

"You have a prime location here."

She followed his gaze to the trail of heavy foot traffic heading toward the hotel-casino's strobing electric-blue lights. "Having Shaw's right next door, it almost guarantees us continuous business."

Calmer rhythms replaced the staccato hip-hop sound beating out of the car's woofers. He aimed an index finger toward the touchscreen display, but she caught his hand, then immediately drew back when his eyes flashed to hers. "Don't change it. I like this song."

Short seconds passed as he shot a glance between her, at the road, and back at her, wearing that inscrutable face, forever shielding him from her scrutiny. "I see you still enjoy dancing. At the reception, you and your boyfriend were out of your chairs for every song."

The car took the Capital Beltway on-ramp and jetted into traffic with lightning speed, the force pinning her back against the seat as her stomach took a nosedive.

With John's influence, they'd paraded about the wedding reception like the happy couple. She was a terrible liar and wanted to come clean, admit that it was an immature ruse, but couldn't make herself do it. She felt foolish enough as it was. And had no answer why other than to make him jealous.

"I meant what I said about discretion. Patrick could try to use it against you in court," he said, now looking straight ahead.

The drive that on any other night would have taken an easy twenty minutes turned into a near hour bumper-to-bumper tango. She tried to initiate small talk, which was just that, a few sentences here and there, while the music helped to fill the awkward quiet between them.

Now parked at her gates, she pressed her keychain remote, then disarmed the house's security alarm from her phone. He rolled through, stopping at the wide front steps. In the time she released her seat belt and gathered her belongings, he'd left the car and held her door open. It was his way—he offered his coat whenever she felt a chill, kept an umbrella above her head on a rainy day, saw to her needs sometimes before she knew she needed it.

He looked up the ten flagstone steps to the double front doors, around at the pristinely manicured lawn, to the rainbow cluster of perfectly arranged flowers, and over at the bubbling fountain centering the grounds. *"This is why we broke up,"* she imagined he had rolling about in his head. He would be wrong. So very wrong.

"I hope bringing me home doesn't put you too far out of your way." There was a sudden tightening of her throat, as she tried to keep the disappointment of what could have been between them out of her voice.

"I'm less than a mile down the road." Silence broke the dialogue for a moment. "I should go. Good night, Evie."

"Would you like some wine?" It was the first thought that came to her to try to keep him there a little longer.

He looked up. "Pardon?"

"I'm going to have a glass. You can join me if you like." She turned away with a casual air, and started up the stairs, hoping he'd follow. Her ringing cell phone stopped her at the door. She fished around in her satchel, and a long breath left her on a weary roll of her eyes skyward. Patrick's calls were a nightly nuisance. "Geez," she grumbled, while stabbing the key into the lock.

"Problem?"

She glanced back. Vincent stood at his opened driver's side door, addressing her over the roof of his car. It was a clear taciturn decline of her invitation. Though expected, his rebuff was no less wounding.

"It's Patrick. I'm not surprised. I ignored his earlier call." She turned away, ready to put it all in her rearview mirror, but she swung around at the sound of a car door slam followed by Vincent's footfalls, heavy and quick, advancing toward her. He took the stairs two at a time to the landing.

"What do you mean he called you earlier? He shouldn't be contacting you at all. If it happens again, I want to know." Frustration flickered in his eyes, but his tone was level.

"Sure," she responded offhandedly on her way into the foyer. "It's just him playing the woe is me card while always finding a way to convey how ungrateful I am."

He followed her inside. "Evie, you need to take this seriously."

"I do take it seriously."

"If you do, why haven't you blocked his number?"

"Because I know him. He'll start calling the bakery. That's my place of business. I can't have that. You have to understand, some of it is clinical with him."

"Not your problem anymore. He has a restraining order against him, which means no contact. That includes phone calls. I'll hang around a bit in case he's foolish enough to come by."

"I told you I don't need a babysitter. You obviously don't want to be here, be near me, so leave."

He frowned. "I never said that."

"You didn't have to. I can see it in your face when you look at me." She slammed her keys and phone down on the round mahogany entry table, then spun on him. "You broke us, damn it!" she shrilled.

His brow shot up, then drew down hard. "Oh, I broke us? I asked you to marry me and you all but said I wasn't good enough for you. You let your mother guide your decision. This—" his arms stretched wide as he turned in a small circle "—this is what you wanted. A mechanic didn't fit the bill. You had no faith in me...in us!"

Her chest constricted with remembered anguish. "My mom didn't like that you dropped out of school. Neither did I." She took a breath to cool her explosive reaction. "Look, I said things that hurt you. I'll own that. But the rest is on you. I'm tired of being the only one wearing the blame. We had a fight. Couples fight. But you walked away and never looked back. You're my attorney, nothing more. We have a business arrangement. If I need a bodyguard, I'll hire one. Now leave."

The door slammed against the frame from the slash of his hand. "You want to know what I think when I look at you?" He whirled her around and pinned her against the hard surface in an instant. His lips descended on hers, crushing, nearly brutal. She struggled against his demanding mouth, but he didn't relent, his tongue snaking deep within and trapping hers, devouring her objection.

She nipped his lower lip and shoved against the steel wall of his chest, breaking the contact. Eyes hard, heavy, her breath sawing out in swift, harsh bursts, she gripped his T-shirt and pulled him down to the slant of her mouth. A guttural moan rumbled deep in his throat as large, strong hands cupped her face, and he kissed her back with a rough, primal insistence. His lips slid down the offering curve of her throat and nipped her skin, repaying the punishment.

She wanted more of it, craved it, starved for it. She whirled him around, shoving him against the solid wood, rebalancing the control, and wrenched up his T-shirt, anxious to lay her hands on his warm skin and the smooth, hard planes of his chest. A heaving sigh left him before he hauled her to him for more savagely urgent kisses.

Each began fumbling with the other's jean zipper, yanking and tugging. In that same haste, she toed out of her flats, then assisted in freeing herself of the constricting denim along with her panties. He spun her, brought up her thigh to his hip, and in one swift thrust, impaled her to the hilt, splintering her into a thousand pleasurable pieces. Their bodies tightly joined, his desire practically glowed from his hot gaze. She shared that same hunger, her blood searing in her veins from the height of her need.

Their lips smashed together, that mind-numbing combination of gentle and violent, not certain who acted first as he hoisted her up by the backs of her thighs and started pumping his hips with determinedly harsh strokes.

Warm breath caressed her neck with each quick exhalation. Eyes closed, she savored the feel of his big body, trembling with each deliciously long sweep of his tongue and flicking of her lobe, while he kept up a nonstop thrusting until, as one, their orgasm struck with a spectacular quivering.

As she waded through the blissful aftershocks that struck her body in intermittent rumbles, he panted heavily against the side of her neck, soft lips brushing her fevered skin.

With it came the reality of what just happened.

The blood started returning to her brain; she eased her legs down from his firm grip and stood on unsteady limbs. He stepped back, blinking rapidly. The look in his eyes, the grooves in his brow, it all read that he'd fully returned from that place of unbridled control, that moment when one got a smack of conscience. It was apparent in his frowning features. She ducked around him to try to cling to a hint of dignity while silence reigned as they quickly dressed.

"This… I don't—" he started.

"You should go." She pulled open the door and kept her eyes averted, not wishing to witness any more of the regret on his face. He stepped out and turned to her, lips pursed to say something. "Good night, Vincent." Evie closed the door and pressed back against it, sliding down to the floor, her mind swimming. She drew her legs to her chest, hugging them tight, and cried into her knees.

Chapter Nine

SUNLIGHT BEAMED ACROSS his face. He didn't recall leaving the bedroom shades up.

Vincent peeled opened his eyelids and squinted. His liquor-stimulated brain struggled to climb out of the cobwebs.

He turned his head to the clock on the nightstand. The bright rays pouring through the window struck what was left of the dark bourbon in the bottom of the bottle and obscured the dimly lit red digits. *Seven something…* He grabbed his phone beside it—twelve after seven.

Last night shouldn't have happened. He'd stepped across that line with Evie, a place no attorney and client should ever venture. But it was so much more than that. *What the fuck was I thinking? Therein lies the problem.* The heightened raw emotions that scraped at the scars left by the wounds she'd inflicted those many years ago found their way to the surface last night. But no sense of closure came following the mind-blinking sex. It brought to mind… *I didn't use a condom. What the fuck!* He palmed the throb pulsing at the crown of his head, cursing himself. Had he lost his damn mind? *But the feel of her. Familiar. Tight. Warm. Potent.* Downing three-quarters of a bottle of Pappy Van Winkle couldn't erase the hot, skin-on-skin friction they'd created.

Jasmine's expected daily text of his schedule yanked him out of his self-inflicted tug-of-war. *Work. Focus on work.* His day showed he was free until the afternoon. He called the office. Jasmine answered within the first ring.

"Good morning, Vincent. Did you get the text?"

"Yes, thanks." He sat up, head a bit wobbly, and brought his legs over the side of the bed. On a test of his equilibrium, he slowly stood. "Connect me to David Grossman." If the man didn't get a handle on his client, Vincent would.

"On it. Just a minute." Music with a nice upbeat Latin tempo hit his eardrum with a punch. He lowered the volume, placing the phone on speaker.

He went into the closet and thumbed through his suits, choosing the faint pinstripes on dove gray. The music cut short just as his brain had started to welcome the lively wake-up pulse.

"Vincent? You there?"

"Yes."

"Mr. Grossman's assistant said he's not in the rest of the week. I got her to share that his schedule has him seeing a friend over golf at Belle Haven Country Club around eight thirty on Sunday morning."

"Good to know." He could always count on her to go the extra mile. "Oh, and Jasmine, let's move my meeting with Mrs. Powell from tomorrow, Friday, to next week. Contact her to see if she's available, say Tuesday morning."

"Your monthly meeting with the partners is that morning, but your afternoon is open. I'll see if she can make it."

"Thanks." They disconnected. Putting space between him and Evie was paramount for his sanity and his career.

Sleeping with a client was never acceptable, no matter if they had a history. To compromise his law practice, destroy all he'd worked so hard to build… He'd made that mistake early on in his career when he'd allowed his damn dick to lead. His partners would surely walk if it happened again. With Evie, narrowing his attention on the job at hand took precedent over his complex feelings for her, starting with him doing some digging on Patrick.

The green was where a lot of business transactions and negotiations took place. He wasn't big into golf, though he kept up his membership at the club.

He scrolled through his contacts and tapped on Dominic's number. The phone rang long enough that he prepped to leave a message, but it connected.

"Vin, my man. What's up?"

There were myriad clinks and the sound of running water heard across the line. "Thought I'd try and catch you before you head to the office. Hope I didn't disturb Tabitha."

"We're up, and I'm headed in after I finish whipping up breakfast for my lovely wife. Mushrooms? What about tomatoes?" Dominic said low. "No, babe, I got this. You sit."

Vincent could hear Tabitha in the background offering to take the reins. The guy adored his wife, treated her like a queen. "Tell Tabitha I said good morning and not to subject that baby to your cooking."

Dominic chuckled. "Tab, Vin said good morning. He also said our son will be lucky to have two great cooks in the kitchen."

"I'm sure he didn't say that," Tabitha responded in a

raised voice, laughing.

"That's cold." Dominic snorted. "So, my brother, what can I do you for?"

"Are you up for a round of golf on Sunday?"

"You hate golf."

"There's someone I need to see. He's spending that morning at the club."

"I'm up for it. What time?"

"Eight thirty."

"That'll work."

"Good. See you then."

After a quick shower and shave, he dressed, then took the spiral stairs that led into the kitchen. Halfway down, the queasiness in his stomach roiled in heavy waves. On any other day, the combined aroma of Clarice's savory hickory-smoked bacon, perfectly seasoned hash browns, homemade buttermilk biscuits, and cheesy grits would have been a welcome start to the morning. But not chasing a whiskey binge.

Warm sunlight flooded the solarium, where laughter and mixed chatter rose between Sasha and an attractive young lady he didn't recognize. As they sat hemmed side by side at the breakfast table with heads hovering over a cell phone, Clarice spooned fluffy eggs onto their plates. Vincent frowned. To argue with his housekeeper that she was not to cater to his sister would be wasted breath. With Clarice's daughter, at age twenty, the same age as Sasha, and stationed in Afghanistan, she'd taken a liking to his sister.

Vincent passed the center island, its marble surface covered with platters of food piled high, on his way to get coffee.

"Good morning." Voices paused. He glanced over his shoulder. The ladies' heads turned almost as one. Clarice's usual warm smile in her cocoa-brown face spread to her kind brown eyes. In contrast, his sister's lukewarm *hello* didn't go unnoticed as she stabbed a fork into her mixed berries. Her disappointment in him for not ordering the cake hadn't waned. But he'd resolved that matter.

The other young lady delivered a long stare with a small curve of her mouth, a gesture recognizable and easily understood. Vincent returned to preparing his coffee. His lips quirked at hearing the young lady's low mutter, "Your brother is so hot." A good reason he paid little to no attention to his sister's female friends.

"What's all this, Clarice? You're supposed to be off today." With cup in hand, he strode to the table and kissed his sister's cheek before circling to an open chair.

"I am, yes." Clarice grinned up at him. "I wanted to prepare breakfast so the ladies leave for their trip to Connecticut on a full stomach. Oh, I'll get them off to the airport as well."

"Appreciate it." Vincent turned back to his sister. "I forgot you're headed to Mom and Dad's for several glorious weeks. I get some peace and quiet. How wonderful it'll be to not have to trip over your belongings," he teased.

Sasha rolled her eyes. "Ha-ha. And before you say anything, we plan to help Clarice clean everything up," she told him and gestured to the young lady beside her. "You remember my friend, Telesha."

"Actually, I don't."

"Of course not," Sasha muttered. "Even though Telesha

and I shared a dorm room sophomore year. Goodness, Vincent, she's been here before."

He remembered only vaguely. Who could keep up with her forever growing friend group? "Oh, right. Yes."

"Hi, Mr. Scott." Her smile still in place, Telesha pushed her braids back over her narrow shoulders, preventing the long tresses from ending up in her bowl of cheese grits, and extended her hand to him.

"Vincent will do." He smiled only politely. "Good to see you again, Telesha."

"You too, Vincent."

Her gaze held steady, her brown-eyed stare unmistakably direct. On that note, he dismissed the overt interest she was pumping at him and took a seat, his brain easily detouring to only one woman. Not that he was comparing. He'd long since stopped trying to find an Evie Langston replica. The one woman who could stop his heart and start it with a simple phrase. Well, she was now Evie Powell and his client.

But her kisses always were able to make him lose all thought, give up complete control. The silky-soft feel of her skin and her unique scent. He wanted more of last night, more of her, and felt like a stumbling addict vying for just one more hit but knew he shouldn't. What happened between them should never happen again. He was her attorney, performing a service.

"Vincent?"

He blinked and looked up from the steam coming off the cup to find Clarice staring at him. "Pardon?"

"I said, is there a problem with your coffee?"

"It's fine." He took a sip.

"You should eat. I'll fix you a plate." Clarice pivoted, forever at the ready to offer aid.

"No, thanks. I'm headed out." He looked across the table at his sister. "I was able to get you that cake."

Sasha's head sprung up from her plate, eyes wide, then narrowing to a side-eyed look of doubt. "Vincent, don't play with me like that. Are you serious?"

"It's all set." He glanced at Clarice's smiling face, who turned to Sasha and nodded. Vincent mimicked his gracious housekeeper's expression. "The order has been placed."

Sasha shrieked, skidded the chair back, and jumped to her feet. She rushed around the table. Long, lean arms enveloped him in a tight hug about the neck, and his cheek was showered with kisses. "Thank you! Thank you! Thank you! I'm going home for the graduation party Mom and Dad are throwing with the family. Then I return here for the real party, and it's gonna be lit."

He chuckled as she danced on her way back to her chair. "Lit in that you will stick to thirty guests. Expect security to check IDs at the door. I'm not getting disbarred for underage drinking. That includes you. In life, you must always set the example. You—" The ring of his cell phone cut into his brotherly sermon.

"Don't follow. Always lead. Yeah, yeah," she mumbled.

"That's right." He grinned as he pulled the device from his pocket. *Evie.* His pulse literally picked up with a tug on his chest. He put the phone away, needing to make sense of last night before he could talk to her. Suppressed feelings that he'd thought were long gone had come loose. He feared what they could do to him if he weren't careful.

"How about we up that number to forty?" Long lashes fluttered sweetly.

Vincent wasn't swayed. "Thirty, Sasha." His voice stern, his terms unyielding, he came to his feet. "Tell Mom and Dad I'll try to visit soon. You ladies be safe."

IT WAS PROBABLY best that he hadn't answered. Evie wasn't completely sure what to say.

She checked her face in the mirror. Eyes red, skin sallow, hair in a tangled topknot—fatigue had a tight hold on her. The entire night, she couldn't shut her mind off. His hard and greedy kisses. His urgent tug on her clothes. The deliciously rough glide of his hands on her body. And when he entered her, the familiar feeling of him, the image of them thrusting, a hard, urgent, pounding pace, the sounds of their panting breaths, a shared heated friction… That euphoric, erotic high stayed with her.

Along with it came the regret, which was what kept her eyes snapping open and staring up at her bedroom's vaulted ceiling skylight. *What was I thinking?* It was also why she felt the best way to move forward was to talk about it. With the phone to her ear, she prepped on what to say to Vincent, but after several rings, she hung up when it went to voicemail.

The sound of Tabitha's car horn sent her dashing about the bedroom. She slipped on her flats, grabbed the darkest pair of sunglasses she had, and hurried out of the house to the car idling at the foot of the steps.

"Sorry. Moving kind of slow this morning. I didn't sleep

well. Mind if we stop at the pharmacy?"

"Sure. What's with the Jackie O look?" Tabitha laughed lightly. "Those glasses are about as big as your face." She stared. "You okay?"

"Yeah. Just need to get something for my headache." It was only party true. She'd been stupidly irresponsible with Vincent last night in more ways than one. Not practicing safe sex was one major bullet at the top of the list.

Tabitha's eyes stretched. "You never take meds. You're feeling that bad? None of your medicinal herb concoctions helped?"

"I-I… Herbs take time to kick in. I need fast relief," she hedged, looking straight ahead. "Busy day, you know. We should get moving. Lots to do."

Tabitha continued to stare at her with long-drawn concern in her gaze. "What's going on with you? Eve, look at me."

She turned her head, feeling safely shielded behind her dark Fendi lenses. "What?"

"You're such a bad liar. Now what's up?"

Evie's cell phone rang. She took it from her satchel and hitched a quiet breath. Vincent's office number. She rushed to open the line. "This is Evie."

"Good morning. This is Jasmine from Mr. Scott's office."

Disappointment and relief shared equal space in the tight anxiety churning in her belly. She slowly let go of the air trapped in her lungs. "Yes."

"Mr. Scott has asked if he could reschedule your appointment from tomorrow to next Tuesday at two o'clock.

Will that work for you?"

"May I ask why?"

"He… There's a scheduling conflict."

A hesitation? Jasmine was covering for her boss. "Next Tuesday at two. I'll be there."

"I'll let him know. Thank you."

Evie stuck her phone back in her bag. "He's avoiding me," she ground out. "It's not like him."

"Who's avoiding you?"

"Vincent."

"Why would Vincent avoid you? He's your attorney."

"We kind of had sex last night." Evie tensed.

Tabitha's eyes stretched wide. "What the hell! And how can you 'kind of' have sex? Never mind, don't answer that."

"I really don't need the lecture right now!" She palmed and stroked fingers at her aching temples. "Can we just go?" Her friend was kind enough to let it be. Whatever reprimand Tabitha had intended likely would've been dead-on, but Evie wasn't in the headspace to listen to sisterly, constructive criticism.

Long, uncomfortable silence settled like a heavy fog on their way to the pharmacy. Tabitha parked at the curb and left the motor running.

"I'll only be a minute." Evie got out and jetted inside. The young cashier greeted her—almost too bubbly at eight fifteen in the morning for Evie's mood. She managed to return a small smile on her swift tread toward the aisles. After finding what she needed, she grabbed a carton of OJ from the refrigerated glass case at the rear, then returned to the still-smiling cashier. The girl glanced up on her swipe of the small box that vividly put on blast Evie's current state of affairs.

"Been there," the girl murmured while making quick work of stuffing the items into a plastic bag.

Their shared circumstance didn't provide much comfort. Perhaps at seventeen it could be called a mistake, a lapse in judgment even. But at thirty-one, it was plain old idiocy at work.

Still hiding behind her dark shades, Evie paid and hurried back to the car. As Tabitha drove to the bakery just a few blocks down and pulled into the reserve spot right out front, Evie tore into to the box and washed down the small white pill with large swallows of the juice, then turned to Tabitha, who was staring at the shredded packaging of emergency contraception. Evie stuffed the evidence of her stupidity into her satchel. "Sorry for snapping at you. You were right. I shouldn't have taken Vincent on as my attorney. But he and I struck an agreement. I intend to follow through with it. All of this, dealing with my divorce and now this thing with Vincent, I'm just a bit stressed."

"I can see that. And Vincent? How does he feel?"

"He still blames me for the breakup. That much I know. As for what happened between us last night, I wish I could explain it. One minute we were arguing, then the next he was kissing me. The rest…"

"Yeah, I get the picture. Obviously, there are some unresolved feelings you have for him, and apparently him for you. Why not explore it?"

Evie blinked. "You were the one who said I should stay away from him."

"That was before you two slept together. You said *he* kissed you?"

"Yes."

"Sex is one thing, but do you still feel something for him?"

Evie nodded, summing up the plain truth of it.

"Then there you go."

Chapter Ten

FUCKING HATE GOLF.

Vincent lay stretched out on the couch as daylight waned to twilight outside his windows and brought in shadows across his living room. He tried his best to move as little as possible while waiting for the muscle relaxers to kick in. He and Dom held David Grossman and his crew through a smooth sixteen holes before Vincent hit the golf ball fat, his club digging in and kicking up thick earth, provoking his body to twist too sharply. All in all, though he'd call chasing after a damn ball a waste of a day, Patrick's attorney hadn't pushed back against just about any offer presented to him.

He reached for his ringing phone on the center table with a teeth-clenching, *"Oof"* brought on from the ache in his right side. "Evening, Evie."

"Vincent."

"I saw you called earlier."

"Twice. Not to mention the messages I've left over the past few days. As my attorney, the least you can do is return my calls."

"Yes, sorry. I've been tied up with work."

"We need to talk. Are you free?"

"Uh, yes."

"Can you come over?"

There were items about her case he needed to share, vitally important matters she should know. To accept her request would constitute as a business meeting, a single-minded purpose, and had only little to do with the deep craving desire to set eyes on her again.

"Vincent? You're there?"

"Yes. Let me take a quick shower." He eased upright, bringing his feet to the floor.

"I'll see you soon."

He made his way upstairs. The meds combined with hot steam helped to relieve the pinch in his lumbar.

He was at Evie's gates just under forty-five minutes. The heavy iron barriers slid open before he could tap the security panel. Bright, perfectly aligned landscape lighting guided him into the driveway. He carefully unfolded himself from the car and trekked up the steps. The door opened to the loveliest face that he'd seen all day as he hit the landing. Her familiar, fresh scent drifted to him on the balmy breeze of the evening. The way her rich-toffee curls were pulled into a thick ponytail drew attention to her high cheekbones. The sleeveless pink, flowy cotton dress exposed arms of lean muscle beneath her smooth skin. The swells of her breasts spilled over the heart-shaped edges of the bodice. The hemline exposed just enough of toned thighs to be a taunting distraction.

"Hey," *beautiful. I'm so screwed.*

"Thanks for coming." She closed the door behind him saying, "I'll just get right to it. You and I…what we did…" Her throat cleared at what sounded like a soft, musical ripple. "That is… As attorney and client, it was inappropriate." She paced a short path, back and forth, chin raised with that scholarly air, glasses slightly lowered along the bridge of her nose, looking utterly adorable. "It's…it's normal behavior for two people such as us who once shared a very strong attraction and a highly charged—"

"Sexual relationship," Vincent put in and rested against the polished round entry table, taking the weight off his right side.

She turned to him. "So, you agree?"

"Yes."

She blinked. "Oh. Good."

He tried not to show the discomfort he was feeling as he straightened from his slouch, but he winced low from the lance of pain that shocked his right side.

Her eyes filled with concern. "Are you okay?"

"Nothing a good night's sleep on a firm mattress won't cure."

"Vincent, what's wrong?"

"I played a round of golf today with Patrick's attorney, David Grossman, and twisted wrong on a swing."

Concern instantly transformed to a look of murderous discontent. "Are you kidding me! You spent the day hanging out with my ex's attorney?" She shook her head. "I can't believe this."

"Evie, listen."

"No, you listen!" she snapped. "Why do you think I fired my last counsel?"

"I'm guessing not because he pulled a muscle playing a sport he dislikes simply so he could try to amicably negotiate on his client's behalf."

She blinked rapidly. "My case?"

He nodded. "Grossman can be a hard-ass and fights dirty. It's known that he lives, eats, and breathes eighteen holes. I, however, wanted to shoot myself today. Be that as it may, I figured Grossman would be amendable on the green. And he was."

"He was?" Her eyes brightened.

"Too accommodating, quite frankly. He said his client would be agreeable to sign over the house, return your vehicle, the paintings, and whatever else he took. Patrick will even surrender his share of your portion of Chase Confections. In turn, you will relinquish your rights to any assets he holds."

"Really!" She beamed. "That's wonderful!" She squealed, and rushed him, arms whipping around his neck as she hauled her warm body against him. "He can keep the car; I don't want it."

Vincent enveloped her at the waist, savoring the closeness. He turned his head to take into his lungs the scent of her fragrant skin before he said, "I told Grossman we'd discuss it, and I'd get back to him with a decision."

She drew back just enough to meet his gaze and kept her embrace loosely locked behind his neck. "Okay. Tell him I said yes to all of it, but he can keep the car."

"I don't think that's wise."

"Why not? Patrick's finally agreeing to something."

"That's the problem. I've handled cases like this long enough to know when I'm being wooled."

"Wooled?"

"It's something my father tends to say—having the wool pulled over one's eyes. In any case, I'd like to look into things a bit more before accepting the terms."

She released him and stepped back, her stare wary, her reverence jerking to a screeching halt. "I don't see the point. Patrick has dragged this out simply to be spiteful. If he's willing to sign off on everything, that's enough for me."

"And it'll happen *after* I'm satisfied there are no landmines. I wouldn't be doing the job you hired me to do if I didn't look out for your best interest. This is me doing just that."

She sighed. "Fine, but don't take too long. Knowing Patrick, he'll back out of it. I want this over and done with."

"Got it. Now, was there something else you wanted, other than your plan to fire me…again?" He smirked.

"Yes. Those things I said long ago… I—"

"I shouldn't have left the way that I did," he jumped in. "It was wrong of me. I'm sorry."

"I'm sorry, too."

A beat of silence settled between them. "Well, I guess I'll head out." He started for the door on a slow drag of discomfort.

"Come." She took his hand and led him into a spacious living room, directing him to sit on one of the three, thick-cushioned couches while she continued to the kitchen. He looked up through the vaulted ceiling skylights to the bright moon in its waning gibbous, and over at the wall of spotless glass. Blue water shimmered in soft waves off the swimming pool, throwing clusters of shadowy brilliance across the flower garden extension of the estate.

Evie returned, holding a towel and something that looked all too familiar—nostalgic—wrapped in linen fabric and tied off with a pink ribbon. "Is that what I think it is?"

"My flaxseed sack." She grinned.

"I remember that. You still make those?"

"Yep, and it's been warmed in the microwave. Now, take off your shoes and lie on your stomach before it cools."

He did as ordered, putting himself in her hands, in her familiar trust. So often, he'd end his night after working at the garage with her tending to his aches.

She kneeled. "Where exactly does it hurt?"

"My lower right side." He lifted his T-shirt and pinpointed the exact spot, eager for her tender ministration. As she worked the heated sack slowly across the sore tissue, followed by her free hand massaging, adding just enough pressure, he fell into a relaxed, foggy daze. Damn, how he missed this, missed her.

"You were always so good at this."

"Undo your belt."

He looked over his shoulder. She didn't blink, clinical in her instruction. Again, he did so, then took up a throw pillow beneath his head, pressing his cheek into the soft cashmere fabric. Clever fingers hooked at his waistband and shimmied his jeans off his hips. Then, for long minutes, she concentrated her efforts just above his right ass cheek. He closed his eyes and relished her attentiveness. The combination of heat and pressure calmed the knotted tendons.

"I'd think your boyfriend would have a problem with this," he murmured into the cloud of his comfort, feeling his eyes grow heavy. "He's a much better man than me if he doesn't take issue with what we did the other night."

"Turn over."

He rolled to his back. With her eyes on his, she unzipped his fly. A gentle yet determined hand slid inside his boxer briefs and freed his dick. Warm fingers circled his length. Slowly. Like torture, that hand began to move up and down with leisurely pumps. Every ounce of willpower he had crumbled. "I'm sure any dude worth his salt would definitely have a problem with this. Damn," he hissed. His voice was a rough, unforgiving quiver.

She smirked, gripping tighter at the base. "He would…if I had a boyfriend."

"You're not dating Tabitha's brother, John?" His breath was quickly growing shallow as he rocked his hips into her now firmly stroking palm.

"John and I are just friends. Do you know him?"

"No," he breathed. That one word said a mouthful, and her lips curved upward.

"Are you checking up on me, Mr. Scott?"

"I asked about him," he admitted, completely not giving a fuck. His dick was so hard, the pressure building so strong, his brain lost all blood supply.

"What about you? I heard you were to bring a date to Kennedi's wedding."

He closed his eyes, unable to think straight. "You heard or you asked?"

"Doesn't matter. Are you seeing someone?"

"No." He latched a hand at the back of her neck, completely lost in the tide, and pulled her down to meet the hard, greedy slant of his lips. His desire quickly set ablaze as their kiss turned to open-mouthed licks and snips, their tongues rolling together in hurried desperation. In that same rushing breath, the palm fisting his shaft sped up, throwing him into a fierce, pounding explosion.

Her hand slowed to a few final, easy strokes. Then she released him, smiling, looking fully aware of her control as she used the towel to clean up the evidence of his gratification.

"How do you feel?"

"Like I could pole vault." They chuckled. "My turn." He slipped a hand beneath her dress, but she shooed away his touch and got up to catch her ringing cell phone over in the kitchen.

"Oh! Mom, sorry, I didn't realize the time. I can't tonight." She locked eyes with Vincent across the wide space. "I have company. No, it's not Tab and Kenni… Stop." Laughter bubbled up as she situated the phone between her chin and shoulder to wash her hands. "I'll catch up on the episode tomorrow… I think the entire world knows you think Shemar's handsome." She laughed. "Geez, Mom, I don't want to know what's happening. You're spoiling it." More laughter.

Vincent recalled how tight the daughter-mother bond had been back in the day. Evidently, it remained as such.

The Langstons had groomed their daughter to be an overachiever. He also knew her parents wouldn't accept her settling for a mechanic. No overt disrespect had been shown him, at least not in front of their daughter. But the message had been made quite clear following a dinner invite as he'd assisted Mrs. Langston with stacking the dishwasher:

"Evie mentioned you like to tinker with cars, that you dropped…decided not to finish college so you could pursue it full-time."

"I chose not to continue school, yes. I'm saving to open my own auto body shop."

"I see. I know you care for my daughter."

"Very much."

"Then you'll understand how important it is that she not become distracted. As I'm sure you're aware, she'll be returning to Brown at the end of her summer break. She's double majoring, carrying a heavy load of classes this coming semester."

"I'm aware. I will drive her back myself."

"Vincent, I know what it's like to let your heart rule. I made that mistake when I was about her age. What I'm trying to say is, I may not have given birth to Evie, but she's a lot like me. I love her more than life itself and will do anything within my power to protect her. Her father and I have worked hard to see that she reaches her full potential, not settle for second best."

Second best. He gave the past a hard shove back behind that tentatively cracked door. Vincent stretched out, sinking into the deep cushions. With eyes shut, the sweet sound of Evie's voice submerged him into a delightfully heavy lethargy.

He dozed, only to awake beneath a soft blanket draped up to his shoulders. Sun pooled in from the window wall and splashed down from the skylights across the marble floor, offering the assurance of a beautiful day. He checked his watch. *Damn.* The time was crawling toward eight a.m. He couldn't recall the last time he'd slept that solid.

The scent of coffee lured him upright, but the beautiful

sight of Evie standing at the counter, sipping from a cup, cleared his morning fog the rest of the way.

She turned her head and smiled. "Morning, sleepyhead."

His chest cinched tight. Why couldn't he resist her? Twelve years and she could still cause his pulse to rush and instantly make his blood heat. He knew he should back away before he sank too deep. Hell, he was barely hanging on by the fingertips as it was.

There had been other woman over the years, but nothing lasted long enough to even hint at something solid. It was as if his soul had been branded, to hunger only for her.

"How's your side? Better?"

"Yes." He got up and was met with only a slight tenderness as he folded the blanket before crossing to the kitchen. Dressed in her signature pale pink Chase Confections T-shirt, hip-hugging jeans, and smelling of fresh berries, she pulled a delicate floral mug from the cupboard.

"I guess I fell asleep. Why didn't you wake me?"

"It's usually so quiet in here. I liked listening to you snore."

"I don't snore." He smirked.

"Please." She chortled. "You more than snore. You call in the cattle."

"Oh, is that right?" He rounded the island in pursuit, but she darted. He pivoted when she tried to run the other way and caught her up into his arms, tickling her into a fit of screeching laughter.

"Okay, okay, you win." She panted, breathless. "If you want to freshen up, there's a small basket of toiletries in the bathroom en suite located in the third bedroom on the right.

I keep it stocked with just about everything for Tabitha or Kennedi. They stay over sometimes."

"Thanks." Vincent made his way to the second floor. He counted seven bedrooms—three to the left, four to the right—plus the master suite's double doors looming at the end of the long, wide corridor. Within bedroom number three on the right was an impressive square-footage bathing in a prism of sunlight. He crossed to the bathroom, quickly washed up, then headed back to the kitchen.

"French vanilla is all I have."

"That'll do." His phone chimed in his front pocket. "Shit." He tapped out a text back to Jasmine.

"Everything okay?"

He glanced up and accepted the cup she offered across the island, taking a good swallow. "I had a client meeting this morning at nine that I forgot about."

"I'm sorry. I should've wakened you last night."

"It's fine. I needed more time to prepare anyway." He sat the cup on the counter and moved to her, curling his arms around her waist, sliding fingers into the back pockets of her jeans for a hearty feel of her firm ass. "Besides, we have unfinished business. I enjoyed last night."

"Me too."

He dipped his head and pressed his nose to the side of her neck, sniffing in her skin. Fresh and delicately sweet, her fragrance easily triggered his need. "I want to taste every part of you." He dragged his mouth upward, nipping along her chin, preparing to feed off her soft lips, but she drew back with a light press of her hand on his chest.

"We shouldn't."

"I know." Yet he returned to kissing the silky glide of her throat, on up to her mouth as she purred. "Just a taste." He hiked up her T-shirt, pushed aside her bra, and buffed the already taut nipples with his thumbs before ducking his head and capturing the pebbled flesh between his lips. With greedy pulls, he sucked, flicked, and brushed kisses where the quick patter of her pulse drummed before latching on to its twin, giving it equal treatment.

"Vincent." Her back bowed encouragingly against his mouth.

As the tip of his tongue traced the under swells of her breasts and dragged lower still, he started to free the button of her jeans, but she leaped away.

"We-we can't," she breathed, rapidly shaking her head.

He was just as labored. The fragrance that was uniquely her drove him with narrow, primal compulsion. Desire stabbed low in his groin, straining behind his fly to near unbearable.

"Not while I'm still in the middle of all this legal stuff."

A scant thread of rational reasoning deep within his blood-deprived brain understood, and he'd set the standard for himself. "Yes, it's bad practice." But right then, the wild pulse drumming in his pants pulsated nearly out of control. The level of want he had for her in that moment outweighed common sense. "You're legally separated. Not to mention, we dated. We've had sex numerous times." The last point was irrelevant but a fact, nonetheless. "That said, you're right." The focus between them had to stay on the task she'd hired him to do.

She grabbed her satchel from the barstool and left the

kitchen while checking her watch. "I need to get to work. Mind giving me a lift?"

"Sure." He filled his chest with air and released a slow breath to tamp down his raging hard-on then followed her out to his car, stepping ahead to catch the passenger door.

"Vincent, I've been thinking," she said when he got into the driver's seat. "Kennedi explained that you filed something called a bifurcation to settle Trent's divorce from his first wife. Maybe you could do the same for me."

He looked at her as he cleared past her heavy iron gates. Attorney-client privilege, he couldn't discuss Trent's case, but the guy went through hell trying to finalize the assets with his ex-wife. "I wouldn't advise it."

"Why not? It would speed things up. Then we could…" She drew her gaze away from his and turned toward her window. "I'd be able to put it all behind me. The bifurcation would do that."

"You'd still have to settle the assets, which could take months, or even longer, depending on your ex's willingness to equitably cooperate. And we know how fair he likes to play." Her head turned to him again. Frustration flushed her face. "As your counsel, I don't advise that. It's a mess on the financial split."

"But I could get closure, sooner rather than later. Your responsibilities as my attorney would be complete. I could move on."

If he were a selfish man, the papers would be in her hands by the end of the day. "Evie, it's my job to protect your interests, see that you get what you're due."

"Yet you don't want to jump on the current offer that

would give me everything I've been wanting right now. Look, I realize that my case is just another number to you. I feel as though my life is on hold. Do you have any idea what that's like? I'm guessing no. Because there are two opportunities that could fix that, but you so easily say hold off on one and a flat no to the other, as if it's no big deal."

To try to reason with her when she was clearly irritated with him would be pointless.

The near twenty-minute drive to Chase Confections offered for an unpleasantly charged silence. He pulled the car up to the curb. By the time he made it around the vehicle to her door, she was practically at the bakery's glass-front entrance. "I can swing by later to take you home, if you like." He reached for her hand, but she jerked it back.

"Not necessary. Have a good day, Mr. Scott." She quickly disappeared within.

Yep, she was pissed at him. As he climbed back into the car and drove off, he brought up on his car's Bluetooth William Drexel, the owner of Drexel Security. William worked for Trent's company, Shaw Enterprise, but Vincent also kept Drexel's expertise on retainer to handle matters at the firm when they cropped up. Like the one he was reaching out about now. The line connected.

"Vincent, this is a pleasure. What can I do for you?"

"Morning, Will. I have someone for you. His name's Patrick Powell."

"You want the usual—financials, background check, surveillance?"

"I'm more interested in his financials. I want to know where every penny he has comes from. I'll send you his profile when I get to the office later this morning. Oh, and I'll need a pretty quick turnaround."

"I'll personally handle it for you."

"Thanks." Vincent paused. "On second thought, provide the full."

"Got it. Reese just finished up a job. I'll assign him to do surveillance. He'll have a tail on Powell by the end of the day. I'll be in touch."

"Great." Something told Vincent that Drexel and his team wouldn't come up empty.

EVIE ENTERED CHASE Confections, hanging on to her annoyance. Had Vincent found the perfect way to get revenge for their past under the guise of a truce? The notion set her entire body humming with suspension. She didn't want to plant that seed, but he was so quick to pump the brakes on two options that would surely benefit her. But he'd also given valid reasons. Damn it, she wasn't sure what to think.

"Morning."

She stopped short and turned toward Tabitha's voice at the round café table stationed before the glass-front window. Across from her sat Kennedi, the cake design binder log opened between them. Evie hadn't noticed them. "Kenni, you're back." She went to them. "How was Rio de Janeiro?"

"Amazing. We plan to go back when we both aren't so busy." Kennedi glanced out the window, then back at Evie, wearing a quizzical stare. "Nice ride."

Evie gave a glimpse through the clear glass and caught the tail end of Vincent's Tesla making a sharp left when the corner traffic light switched to green. She gestured at the binder. "Glad you both are here. As you can see, the schedule is jammed with orders this month."

Both cut smooth grins. "Don't even play. Spill it," Kennedi said. "You and Vincent? I haven't been gone that long."

Evie looked around at the customers seated about, many with heads buried in their electronic devices, and the staff tending to tables nearby. "There's nothing to tell. He gave me a ride to work," she said low and strode off, making her way to their back office, knowing Tabitha and Kennedi would follow.

"He gave you a ride to work. How nice of him." Tabitha smirked and closed the door. "Oh, that reminds me. I got you something." She went to the locker, pulled from her purse a small plastic bag, and handed it over before taking a seat on the couch. "Wouldn't want you to have a repeat of before."

Evie looked inside. "Condoms?" She stared. "Really, Tab?"

"Magnums." Tabitha winked. "I took an educated guess."

"Obviously, I've missed a lot. Ladies, tea please. Fill me in." Kennedi grinned.

Evie sighed. "I asked Vincent over last night to clear some things up." She stuck the condoms into her satchel then moved past their determinedly grounded stances to grab an apron from the wall hook.

"He spent the night and…?" Kennedi asked.

"We fooled around a bit." No need to go into more than that. Evie felt she'd tipped the teacup just enough to placate them. "He fell asleep on the couch."

"You looked upset when you got out of his car," Tabitha remarked matter-of-factly and stood. "Kennedi and I saw the exchange between you two."

"Vincent played golf yesterday with Patrick's lawyer…" Catching Tabitha's deep frown, she explained, "He said it was to negotiate my case. That wasn't the issue. When I asked him to speed things up by doing for me what he'd done to expedite Trent's divorce, he said he didn't think it's a good idea. Sex is off the table until that happens. But more importantly, I'm not sure I can trust that he's over what happened in the past between us."

"Wait. You did or didn't sleep with Vincent?" Kennedi's brow crinkled with confusion.

"Kenni, keep up. Evie slept with Vincent but not last night."

"Ah." Kennedi nodded. "Evie, I have to agree with Vincent. He filed a bifurcation of divorce for Trent, which dissolved the marriage with his ex-wife, but it took years for the two to settle the assets. It can get very messy. I'm talking ugly. Trent had an apartment in Paris, one he owned before the marriage. His ex-wife insisted he include it in her settlement. When he did, she still refused to sign, saying she wanted him to include the cost for monthly upkeep. And that's just one example. I have plenty. My point, she found excuse after excuse to drag out the settlement."

"Eve, remind you of anyone?" Tabitha asked.

"You should listen to Vincent; he's doing his job," Kennedi advised.

"Well, ladies, I'm only here until noon. We should get started on some of these orders if you don't want to be here all night." Tabitha drew open the door. "Evie, sweetie, don't be so hard on yourself. You've been separated for a year. If you care for Vincent, which I know you do, stop with the ridiculous 'no sex until the ink dries' craziness. You know you want to jump his bones," she said quietly but in her usual direct way, smiling on her stroll out.

Chapter Eleven

*W*HAT THE…!

A romantic comedy or music to groove to, good food to pig out on, bottles of delicious wine to kill, and lots of dirty guy talk. Evie had been looking forward to hanging out with her girlfriends for the monthly ladies' night all week. No men allowed was the rule. So why when she strode happily into Kennedi and Trenton's lavish, two-story penthouse apartment was she met with the high volume of the TV blaring ESPN SportsCenter? She took the two steps down into their living room only to find Dominic and Trenton helping with dinner prep over in the kitchen.

"Hey, you made it," Tabitha called from her spot among them at the island counter while she tossed a bowl of fresh field greens.

Evie blinked out of her surprise and tried not to let the annoyance roll in. The men's heads pivoted to her across the room, each offering hellos. As the guys continued boisterous sports commentary while completing the tasks Tabitha had, no doubt, assigned them, Evie pulled opened the fridge to put away the wine she'd brought. She used the moments shielded behind the subzero stainless steel to mouth silently to Tabitha, "What are they doing here?"

"Sauvignon Blanc. Perfect pairing for the garlic salmon."

Kennedi's voice made Evie pivot toward the dining room. Pretty flowers in a heavy crystal vase were staged in the center of the large round glass table. Tea candles flickered among the fine plate settings and wine goblets. The floor-to-ceiling sliding glass doors were open wide, showcasing underneath the cloudless, starry night D.C.'s brilliant cityscape across the Potomac River. It all looked so beautiful, Romantic. But… *Are you kidding me!*

Ladies' night in was about chowing down, sprawled out on the floor in stretchy sweats. Evie looked down at her yoga pants and well-worn Brown University alma mater T-shirt topped off with tan slippers. She hadn't even bothered to don shoes. It was *ladies'* night in, damn it.

"Evie, bring over the wine. I have the ice bucket filled," Kennedi beckoned from the dining table extravagance.

She walked over and handed off the bottles. "Why are your husband and your brother-in-law here? Did you forget to tell Trent we had plans tonight?" she whispered.

"Tab and I thought it'd be nice to invite the guys, just this once."

The console on the wall in the kitchen chimed. Trenton tapped a button and spoke to the security guard down in the lobby. "Vincent is on his way up."

Evie's eyes went wide. She swung her head back to Kennedi. "You invited Vincent?"

"Yes. You guys can hang out…talk. What better way than with friends?" Kennedi smiled sweetly.

Tabitha brought to the table the bowl of salad greens with goat cheese garnish.

Evie glared between them. "I see you're in on this, too. What happened to sistahood?" she said low as she heard the entry door open and shut. She peered into the kitchen and witnessed the men greet Vincent with gripped palms and bro hugs. The trio easily fell into sports talk about various highlights that were still roaring out of the surround sound. "You guys are supposed to have my back."

"We do have your back. That's what this is about." Tabitha draped an arm around her shoulders, drawing her close. "Straight talk, girlfriend—"

"As if there were any other kind with you." Evie's irritation was now unapologetically front and center.

Tabitha shrugged. "True. You know you still have feelings for the guy. And I'm guessing he does for you, too. All this talk about waiting until after things are finalized with your ex—things have been over for more than a year. You deserve happiness. Now, stop being mad." Her arm cinched them closer, expressing a friendship that stood above all else. "Look at him—tall, broad, and broodingly hot." They angled their heads and stole a glimpse over at the men now gathered around the TV, debating like commentators. "If you don't snatch that brother, some lucky woman will, for sure."

"We're just trying to help a little." Kennedi's hand clasped hers.

Evie gave another glance at Vincent, catching the deep rumble of his chuckles among his buddies. He was indeed all that. Still, she simply didn't like not being privy to the plan, even if Tabitha and Kennedi were looking out for her. Ever since they'd started dating Dom and Trent, and now they were related by marriage, it seemed to bond the two even closer. She felt herself getting shoved out of the sista circle. An outsider. "You should've told me. I could've at least worn something appropriate for your *fancy* dinner party."

"Fancy?" Kennedi waved a hand between them. "We're all practically wearing the same thing."

"I can hardly fit into anything else." The roundness of Tabitha's extended belly stretched the cotton tee a bit beyond its limits. "Sweetie, you look fine. More than fine. You're beautiful." She tucked unruly frizzy hair back into Evie's loose top bun.

Her annoyance with them had softened considerably, but she couldn't let them get off that easy. "Whatever. I'm here now."

The oven timer beeped, pausing everyone's conversations. Kennedi hurried off.

Evie followed her friends and was met by brown eyes, the color of rich warm whiskey, tracking her stroll into the kitchen. He was most definitely eye candy. A catch.

"Hi, Vincent." His smile took her breath away as he circled the island to her. And, man oh man, he smelled so yummy, like clean shaving soap after a fresh shower.

"Evening, Evie. I was hoping I'd see you, though I have to admit, I hadn't expected you'd be here." Strong fingers curled around her hand that rested on the counter, his thumb stroking her knuckles. "Can we talk later?"

Her nerves twisted into tight knots. That feeling a girl got when a guy she liked finally approached and asked to hang out and chat but wasn't one hundred percent sure it'd be what she wanted to hear. "If it's about filing the bifurcation, I've changed my mind."

"It was about that, yes, and some other things. I want—" Dominic delivered a slap on Vincent's back, and he turned. "Dude, really?"

"Let's eat. I'm starved."

"When are you not?"

Damn it, Dom. Talk about poor timing.

Everyone grabbed a dish. Garlic butter baked salmon, vegetable risotto, sauteed balsamic zucchini slices and warm rolls were brought to the table.

Vincent already had Evie's chair extended. Her gaze rose to his with a fondness that swelled like a rushing, warm wave. "Thanks."

"You're welcome."

Laughter, easy conversation, and playful teasing blanketed the table. The couples would make up for their lighthearted jabs at their spouses with a quick peck on the lips now and again. A small twinge of jealousy jabbed through Evie's common sense. Even if she were still with Patrick, he'd never have joined her at a get-together with her friends. For one, he said Kennedi and Tabitha were a bad influence. Some of the blame for the separation was cast on her girlfriends. *Not.*

The joking didn't let up as everyone pitched in to do cleanup.

"Is there space for one more?"

She straightened from stacking the dishwasher and took the plate Vincent held out to her. "I'll make it fit. Anything else before I start it up?"

He looked around the now-spotless kitchen. "I think

that's it." His big body leaned back against the counter with arms folded at his chest, provoking the bulk of muscles to jut even more. "I hear you ladies hang out like this once a month."

They both gave a glance at their friends now lounging on the couches over in the living room, laughing it up. "We do, but it's a lot less formal. Hence..." She raised a foot, showing off her comfy slipper. "We're usually in our pajamas."

Brow low, he regarded her for a moment, his expression amused, even mischievous. "I would've been up for that." With a smile, he leaned in close, his voice dropping. "I've always liked the look of you in your pj's. If I recall, it's panties and nothing else. Has that changed?"

Her cheeks flushed hot. His flirtatious whisper caused a little jump in her pulse. "Well, I tend to wear a bit more for sleepovers."

He sucked his teeth and rolled a shoulder, resuming his relaxed pose. "I take it you weren't given the heads-up that us boys would be crashing your party, which leads me to ask, had you been told *I'd* be here, would you have shown?"

"I guess we'll never know." She smiled back. "You were going to say something earlier."

"Hey, Vin and Evie, we're about to play truth or dare."

Damn it, Dominic! Evie prickled once again over his awfully poor timing. She looked at Vincent, who shrugged. "I guess we're playing."

They joined the group and took a seat together on the couch.

"I'll go first." Dominic leaned forward, starting things off with a sly smile at his brother. "Trent, truth or dare?"

Trenton looked down at Kennedi seated on the floor between his split legs, and she met his gaze. He pressed a kiss upon her brow, then addressed his brother. "Truth."

"Okay. What is the one thing you'd never do, not for all the money in the world?"

"Hmm. Good question." Trenton scratched his chin. "I'll never stop loving my wife, not for all the money in the world."

A roar of boos followed by a hail of throw pillows pummeling Trenton.

"Ignore them, babe." Laughing, Kennedi hooked a hand behind her husband's head and pulled him down for a kiss, their affection unashamed.

"All right." Trenton grinned. "Evie, truth or dare?"

"Dare."

"I dare you to share your most awkward moment."

"My most awkward moment." Evie sat back. It came to her in an instant. "Uh, give me another question."

A burst of objections rang out. She really didn't want to say it. When Vincent looked her way and his lips curved upward, she had a strong feeling he knew. "Trent, maybe you really should try another question," she said.

"No changes," Dominic hooted and received support from the others.

"Fine." She glanced at Vincent again, then around at the group. "My most awkward moment was walking in on your parents making out in the coat closet at your wedding."

The room fell pin-drop silent for a long stretch. Then, everyone started talking at once.

"No way." Dominic rapidly shook his head. "It's impossible you saw our mom and dad getting busy. They can hardly stay in the same room for a minute without arguing."

"What Dom said," Trenton added.

"Well, they were in full agreement on smooching when I saw them." Evie sniggered.

"I witnessed it as well." Vincent chuckled.

Dominic and Trenton's faces remained frozen before they broke into riotous laughter that spilled across them all. As they settled down, Evie turned to Vincent, "Truth or dare?"

"Um, truth."

"You once loved restoring cars, even left college to focus on your passion. Why did you decide to finish school and become an attorney?"

He sat forward, elbows on his knees, then looked back at her, a tightness setting in the strong angle of his jaw. "Joe Hodge's garage caught fire. It burned to the ground so fast, the firehouse that was only about a block away hardly got a chance to run the hose."

"No!" Evie's hand flew to her mouth. That poor, scruffy, sometimes cantankerous old man she knew Vincent held in high esteem. Hodge's Custom Auto and Repair—its shiny red tow truck rescued her from the side of the road and linked her to the man seated beside her. So many moments she'd shared with Vincent at the garage—some wonderful, some bittersweet, some hurtful.

"Was he okay?"

"Long story short, Joe's attorney was a swindler. Not only did he suck at his job, but he also took Joe for every penny he had."

She'd anticipated he'd say she was the reason he pursued a law degree. The last conversation they had was about that very topic before he walked out of her life. Turns out, it had nothing to do with her. No longer did she have to carry the weight that she'd been the catalyst to him giving up his passion, leaving a path he enjoyed.

"I'm sorry, Vin. I know how much you loved it there. The shop held a lot of great memories for me, too. It played a significant part in how we met. I cherish that." He sat back. In his steady gaze, she saw that he shared those words.

"I became an attorney to help people like Joe. Twenty to thirty percent of my firm's caseload is pro bono work."

A profound appreciation swaddled all the fervor she felt for him, like an all-encompassing tornado sweeping her up, throwing her forward, and dropping her down, offering her a second chance for happiness. If he'd allow it. Evie touched his arm, needing to express her affection in some small way, long past caring that they had an audience. "That's really wonderful of you, Vin."

"My turn," he said softly. "Truth or dare?"

"Truth."

"Would you date a hardworking yet struggling mechanic?"

Evie held his sharp gaze. The entire room maintained a pulsing quiet, their friends watching closely. "I would, if the man were honest, decent, didn't judge me for who I once was, and accepts me for who I am today."

"Have dinner with me."

"We just had dinner."

He smiled. "Not now. How about next Friday?"

"Okay." She turned to a smiling Kennedi, then shifted a look toward Tabitha, who was also grinning. "Tab, truth or dare?" Evie asked, drawing everyone back into the game. Though all she could focus on was what to wear for her date with the beautiful, caring man beside her.

Chapter Twelve

"JASMINE, I'M HEADED to lunch then to a meeting. I likely won't be back," Vincent said on his stride to the elevator.

"This just came for you from Mr. Grossman's office."

He pivoted and took the legal envelope she handed him. It had been agreed that Vincent's firm would prepare the Powell v Powell documents. He sat his briefcase on the floor and pulled out the papers, prepared to skim the terms they'd verbally worked out during that hellish game of golf.

What the fuck? Instead, the petition for divorce cited adultery in clear, black font. "Is he serious?" he barked.

"Is who serious?"

Vincent looked up to see Sloane approaching. Their other partner, Winston Wardell, was a few paces behind her. Sloane claimed Winston had a Bradley Cooper look about him. Vincent didn't see it. What he had noticed lately was the two had been finding ridiculous reasons to assist one another on their cases, often a lot of late nights spent together in the company's documents library. He didn't raise the issue, since, so far, their clandestine romantic involvement didn't interfere with the partnership.

"We were going to ask if you wanted to join us for

lunch." Sloane leaned in to get a look at the document, then up at Vincent. "Evie Powell. Did you know?"

Winston gave a look. "That takes away your leverage to negotiate." He always had the tendency to state the obvious.

Vincent gestured over at the small glass-front meeting room opposite the receptionist desk, and the partners followed him inside. He closed the door. "This is clearly Mrs. Powell's ex trying to find a way to get out of forking over what he owes her." But the allegation was indeed true…and Vincent played a significant starring role. If it got out, even in speculation, it could potentially harm the firm; he could lose everything.

"The man is abusive to his wife." That was also true. "I'm going to have a talk with Grossman."

He needed to get a handle on this. Though there wasn't any mention of him in the petition, it wouldn't take much for that to change.

VINCENT CAME OUT from underneath the hood of his sister's Mustang and grabbed the towel from the front bumper to wipe his hands before pulling his ringing phone from his back pocket. "It's Evie." He went back to replacing the filter.

"You're going to ignore her?" Trenton rested back against the metal tool cabinet and sipped his beer.

"I need to get this done." He lifted the intake hose to get to the air box.

"I'm not talking about that. You have dinner plans with

Evie Friday."

Vincent glanced up. "I received the papers today from Patrick's attorney." He shared with Trenton the circumstances of the petition and his role in it. "I'm going to cancel the date." Damn, he didn't want to but saw no other choice. "I managed to get Grossman to understand that his client is a fucking liar and that I have proof of abuse. I explained that I went to meet with my client at her place of business and came upon the assault firsthand. That I had to intervene. There are cameras on every block of the Wharf. Grossman understood it would be easy to prove and the potential harm it could do. We're back on track with the originally negotiated terms. I don't want to fuck it up. My firm is on the line as well if I do."

"Yeah." Trenton crossed his legs at the ankles and tipped up his bottle, taking a long swallow. "It's seven forty on a Wednesday night. I'm here at my attorney's house to go over the docs for the investment meeting next week. But you're under the hood doing maintenance on your sister's car, and I'm on my second beer. My point—you can make arrangements to meet with Evie that would *appear* well within reason to discuss her case."

"We met briefly at my office yesterday to go over the particulars. I kept it professional. There's no need to meet further. Our going out can't happen."

"Who said you have to stay local? The country is vast, my brother, and you have the means."

Vincent met his stare. Both shared subtle smiles.

Chapter Thirteen

"I HAVE NOTHING to wear."

Wrapped in a bath towel, Evie stood before her wardrobe. Every outfit was less appealing than the last. She glanced back at Kennedi and Tabitha seated on the chaise. "Ladies, help me out here. And what the heck am I going to do with this hair? It's a frizzy mess. Vincent will be here in an hour, and I'm nowhere near ready. Maybe I should reschedule. It's not like he bothered to call all week. Sure, we talked about my case on Tuesday, and I got a text from him late Wednesday. Only after I called and texted first." She paced. Anxiousness twisted her stomach into knots. She hadn't been on a date in more than eight years. "What if he's having second thoughts? We did agree to keep things between us professional. Research has determined that spontaneous decisions are oftentimes second-guessed a day later."

Both ladies got up and came to stand to the left and right of her.

"You're not canceling. He's probably swamped with work," Kennedi reassured her. "He's running a company; you know how that can be."

"Let's see." Tabitha sifted through an array of cocktail

dresses, beautiful fabrics in chiffons, silks with beaded tulle overlays, crepe satins, and soft velvets. "What do you mean you don't have anything to wear? I count like thirty or so to choose from." She pulled down a black cross-shoulder clingy option. "What about this one?"

Kennedi caught the tag hanging from the dress's side seam. Her eyes widened. "Five hundred forty dollars! It's never been worn!" She flipped through several others in mint condition.

"I won't wear them." Each one carried an unpleasant imprint on Evie's memory, a token to atone for an abusive touch or vicious words. "They're gifts—" hard air quotes "—from Patrick. I plan to donate them."

Kennedi shoved it back on the rack, not too gently. "I know just the dress you can wear. I'll run home and be right back."

"What dress?" Evie called as Kennedi hurried out.

"Don't worry about it. We got you." Tabitha ushered her to the vanity and guided her into the chair, then grabbed the hairbrush. "Now, let's lock these curls."

As Tabitha went to work taming strands, Evie put in her eye contacts and applied her makeup.

When the security chimed sometime later, Tabitha dashed off to view the monitor in the bedroom, then returned. "It's Vincent. Kennedi is rolling through the gates right behind him. I'll go down and keep him company."

The clock showed he was fifteen minutes early. She put on matching lace bra and panties, then spritzed on a bit of perfume.

Kennedi entered carrying a garment bag. "Here you go."

Evie quickly slipped into the silky red dress that hugged her body, hitting mid-thigh. The V-shaped bodice cut so low it just about reached her navel. She turned in front of the full-length mirror to view the back that exposed even more skin. "You call this a dress? How am I to wear a bra in this thing?"

"You don't need it." Kennedi unhooked the back lace, tugged, and freed her of the delicate material. "Your girls can hold their own. Here." She took from the shelf the black leather pair of Manolo Blahnik pumps and guided Evie's feet into the severe arches. "There, you're all set."

After stuffing her clutch with the essentials, Evie gave herself one more look in the mirror. Her curls were popping. Her skin gleamed. Her makeup wasn't overdone.

"Vincent is waiting. And, girlfriend, he looks good. Really good." Kennedi grinned. "Now go."

On a long, bracing breath, Evie made her way downstairs.

"There she is," Tabitha said, and Vincent turned.

"Hey. Sorry for the wait." She regarded the way his brow lifted ever so slightly as his gaze stroked over her. A small smile spread across his lips. Black shirt beneath a dark gray suit, he indeed looked smoking hot.

"It was worth it. You look amazing."

With warmth rushing into her cheeks, she spoke to her two champion sisters. "Lock up for me?"

"We got it," Tabitha said, smiling.

"Have fun." Kennedi winked.

Out front, the driver, Jim, stood at the rear open door of the idling limo. As they settled within and the vehicle cleared the gates, Evie turned to Vincent. Sandalwood and spice. The pleasant aromatic fragrance of his cologne drifted, teasing her nose, distracting her for a moment. But it was so much more that remained a stamp on her memory. Her attraction to him, which hadn't diminished after all the years apart, was an intoxicating pull that coiled her into a constricting knot of yearning. She'd satiated his lust the other night on her couch while denying her own. The mere sight of him tonight started a fever building in her blood instantaneously.

"Where are we having dinner?" she asked as her gaze explored his handsome face, on down the broad expanse of his exceptional physique, feeling almost desperate to press her lips to any area of his exposed skin. His reply was interrupted by the buzz of his cell phone.

"Excuse me." Brows drawn close, his thumbs rapidly tapped out a reply to whoever had affected his mood and took precedence in that moment. When he looked at her again the frown hadn't left his face.

"Something wrong?"

In a blink, his features reverted to smooth, appealing angles. "This damn graduation party will be the death of me. Sasha's in Connecticut, hanging out with her old high school friends. Now she wants to add to her forever growing guest lists."

"How many more?"

"Seven. Next Saturday can't come fast enough," he ground out.

"That's not a lot. I always increase the portion size slightly to account for situations like this. It shouldn't be—" This time it was his phone ringing that interrupted their evening.

"I really need to get this. It'll only take a minute."

The seriousness in the depths of his eyes as he listened to the caller made the hairs on her arms stand up before he turned away. "Will, are you certain?" she heard him say. When his call ended, he stared out, unblinking, his peculiar mood indiscernible.

"Everything okay?"

"Just work. Now, what were we talking about?"

She didn't push the matter. An attorney, he likely held a cellar of secrets. "I asked, where are you taking me for dinner?"

"I see you're still not a fan of surprises."

"I didn't know it was a surprise." Droplets of rain hit the window and came more steadily as the car took the Capital Beltway on-ramp leading out of the city. "Hope you brought an umbrella. It's about to come down pretty hard." *Bummer.* A clear, starry evening would've sealed the night in her fairy tale.

Warm fingertips gently caressing along her arm drew her attention away from the impending downpour. His eyes were fixed on hers, piercing, and he moistened his lips, conveying an unmistakable want. To test her theory, she crossed her legs, letting the soft fabric ride up and his gaze shifted there, lingering, then back to hers. It gave her a bit of confidence, but more, it proved with satisfaction that the sensual vibe in the air was mutual. His hand came to rest on her thigh and found its way beneath her dress, fondling just shy of her apex, toying with the lace trim of her thong. He inched closer. Soft lips brushed her bare shoulder, sweeping up the contour of her neck. She heard him breathe her in slow and deep as he nuzzled and tasted her skin.

"I've always loved your scent."

"Vincent." She swallowed to suppress the tremendous urge to spread her legs, to let him stroke her passion nerve raw, slake the aching knot that was suddenly pulsing and close to undermining her control. "Looks like the rain will ruin our evening," she voiced on a quiet pant as his fingers breached the thin veil and easily found its target.

"Behave, Mr. Scott." She shifted over slightly, breaking contact, needing to douse the flames that started to burn from the inside out. It was either that or give in to the delicious torture that would turn her into a panting, wailing puddle of quivering flesh and certainly alert the driver to their naughty escapades.

"For now." He grinned, sat back, and adjusted the bulge in his pants, unabashed, proving he'd been just as affected. "By the way, you won't be needing an umbrella. Last I checked, Vegas's skies are clear."

"We're going to Vegas?" He gestured a nod at her window. The car hooked a right onto the DCA terminal access point, drove down a long, brightly twinkling stretch of road, then headed straight for a private jet waiting on the tarmac, and came to a stop. Jim, holding two opened umbrellas, pulled open the car door. He handed one to Vincent, who ushered her up the stairs and into the aircraft's cabin.

"Good evening," the steward greeted. "Can I start you off with a glass of wine or champagne?"

"Spence, good to see you." Vincent turned to Evie. "What would you prefer?"

When in Rome... "Champagne."

Luxury leather couches, wide reclining chairs, and glossy maplewood veneer replaced standard row, narrow seating. Evie took it all in as they sat opposite one another at a white cloth table elegantly dressed in fine china and heavy sterling silverware. The steward, Spence, brought a bottle of Dom Perignon and filled their glasses. When he retreated, she sipped a good bit of the bubbly and eyed Vincent over the rim as he nearly emptied his.

"A private jet?"

"The perks of having a best friend who owns a Gulfstream." He leaned in; even a hint of grin managed to heighten his easy good looks. "It's Trent's company plane. He travels often from D.C. to his corporate office in Vegas. As his attorney, so do I. But I thought it best that we not hang out in the DMV."

"Because we might be seen together." She'd determined the motive for his little excursion the second she saw the big metal bird geared up and waiting for them.

The door to the galley opened, drawing their attention. Out came Spence rolling a dinner cart with warm breadsticks, portioned bowls of salad greens, and covered dishes. Given the night so far, Evie predicted a finely cut filet or a perfectly seared fish hidden beneath the sterling silver domes. Instead, the fancy lids were removed to reveal—

"Vegetable lasagna with extra mushroom," Spence announced as he served up the steaming hot, cheesy, stacked layers of pasta. "Will there be anything else?"

"No, thanks," Vincent said.

"Enjoy."

Alone once again, she stared down at her plate. The rich aroma of sweet garlic and basil filled her nostrils, a complete one-eighty of what she'd expected. The choice entrée pushed at the door of her cherished memories.

He reached across the table and curled his fingers around her hand, gently stroking her palm. "Extra mushrooms are still your favorite, I hope."

"Yes."

"It's what we had on our first date. I'm sure the chef did a much better job than my attempt back in the day." He chuckled lightly.

"Yours was burnt on the bottom." She looked up. Her heart swelled so heavy she could hardly withstand the pressure, unable to find her words. She left her chair, settled on his lap, and circled her arms around his neck, crushing her lips to his with warm familiarity. Unashamed, her kisses were hard and deep and wanting. "You remembered."

"I've never forgotten you, Evie Langston." Warm fingertips charted along her cheek. Each brush was gentler than the last as his eyes gazed deep into hers.

"Are we flying back home tonight?"

"That's up to you. I keep a suite at Shaw-Vegas where I stay when I'm in town."

She claimed his lips again, unhurriedly this time, dropping all barriers, and felt his hand travel slowly up her thigh, tunneling beneath her dress. He gave her buttocks a firm squeeze. The other hand slipped inside the bodice and caressed her breasts as their tongues mated. She settled into his demanding kisses that were equal parts soft and hungry and hot amid his exploring touches reacquainting with her body. When she forced herself to break away from the heat of his lips once more, she got up, but he caught her hand.

"One more kiss." He stood.

"I'm going to ruin my hair and makeup."

His eyes roamed over her. "You look smoking in that dress." His hand still holding hers, he tugged, and she followed him into a room at the back of the plane. The light flickered on. Decked out among the furnishings was the most enticing, full-sized bed draped in crisp white sheets, fluffy pillows, and a cashmere blanket.

"Vincent." As much as she wanted to sprawl out with him upon that thick mattress, she shook her head. "We can't. If you knew what it took to get this hair to—"

His mouth claimed hers while he backed her up against the closed door, chipping away at her narrow control. He dropped his head between the exposed swells of her breasts. The severe vee made his exploration in capturing a nipple quite easy before he trailed a hot path lower still on his way to his knees.

He looked up, connecting his gaze to hers, molten in his steady stare. "I want to taste you."

The smoldering look in his eyes mixed with the flash of his devilish grin. She nearly lost the will to breathe as his warm fingers caught the delicate band of her panties and slid the lacy material down her legs, freeing her sex of the thin barrier. She bucked at the first swipe of his tongue over her clit, his caresses slow and controlled, driving her to distraction. Then, with an aggressive purpose, his mouth took her greedily, sucking and licking her pussy with a nonstop motion. He caught her left leg and brought it to his shoulder, allowing him to pierce her narrow passage with his tongue, spearing her over and over, like stoking a flame. As he took his fill, she threw her head back and planted her hands flat above her head against the cool, hard surface, searching for purchase to stay upright, panting in wanton, heightened ecstasy. She grew light-headed, feeling she might pass out with each quick then slow swirl of his tongue. Not since Vincent, past and now present, had she been pleasured in such a way. Her ex didn't assent to certain erotic explorations; his austere orderliness had crippled their intimacy.

Right there, she breathed heavily, so close to exploding. Her hand latched on to the back of his head, holding him steady. The quaking started deep in her core then bloomed wide, striking every humming nerve ending. She couldn't stifle her cry as her orgasm racked her entire body. He didn't let up, his mouth continuing to devour her, his greedy licks switching to torturous swirls before he eased up and came to his feet. His tongue swept over hers, kissing her deeply, sharing her female heat.

"If I recall, I had my dessert before dinner that night long ago, too," he murmured as he sucked in her shallow breaths. "You're as sweet as I remembered."

Her bones were wobbly within her skin; she could barely move without stumbling. "Wh—" She swallowed and sucked in oxygen to refuel her brain. "Where are we going in Vegas?"

"We have reservations to see Cirque du Soleil's *Zumanity*."

"I've heard of it. It's gotten high marks." With the feeling returning to her extremities, she attempted to straighten her appearance. "Our dinner is getting cold. Fair warning, that garlic is going to be potent," she teased while slowly regaining her bearings.

He directed her attention to the door on the opposite side of the room and retrieved her panties from the floor. "Disposable toothbrushes, toiletries, everything you need is in the lavatory."

She stepped away from his temptingly beautiful, tall form. "I'll be out in a minute." With a light hold of her chin, he tipped her head up and kissed her tenderly, sweetly. When the door closed, she pressed her body back against it to catch her breath. He was so much male, so alluring, so potent.

She hadn't forgotten him either.

VEGAS'S NEW YORK, New York Theater's VIP section allowed for comfy couch-style seating with an up close and personal view of the stage. They sat intimately close, his heat deliciously scorching the areas of her exposed flesh. A waiter asked if they'd like something from the bar, but both declined.

As the lights lowered, he relaxed an arm along the spine of their shared seat, easily tucking her in against his big body.

Fingers, featherlight, toyed in her hair at the nape of her neck and gently caressed along her bare shoulder. Every maddening brush intensified that wild, hot current. She turned her head and met the slow curving of his lips that set alight a smoldering flicker of heat in his eyes.

"Cold? Your arms have goose bumps." He peeled out of his suit jacket and wrapped it about her shoulders. "That should help." His attention returned to the stage while his hand resumed its sweet, sizzling touches, as if knowing precisely which nerve to taunt.

For the next hour and a half, the topless acrobats, the dancers, the contortionist, the entire titillating erotic cabaret mesmerized the audience, Evie included.

The provocative stage performance only heightened her yearning.

Finally, they stood in Shaw Hotel and Casino's private elevator with one other couple as it carried them upward. The bell dinged on the thirty-third floor. The couple stepped off. The second they were alone, Evie spun and captured Vincent's mouth with hers, unable to hold back a second longer. She looped her arms around his neck and his circled her waist, drawing her tight against his body. "I've wanted to do this all night," she said between their shared breathless kisses.

"That makes two of us." He cupped her breasts. Her pulse punched beneath his large palms.

Another ding, and the doors parted. He backed her out of the elevator and crossed to the suite without breaking their fierce lip-lock. Warm lips kissing behind her ear only made her hotter, achier, and ready. "Vin, we should get out of the hallway."

The latch clicked, and they practically fell together inside. He came at her, taking her mouth in a mad hungry rush as he kicked the door closed and once again hemmed her up against it.

His fingers sank into her hair. Hot lips scorched a trail along her cheek, chin, and neck, teasing her flesh with light nips and licks. She yanked at his shirt, freeing buttons in haste, and wrenched the fabric out of the waistband of his slacks to run her hand over the broad terrain of solid muscle.

"Vincent," she stammered, breathy, feeling his teeth repeatedly graze her nipple as he moved back and forth from one stiffly peaked knot to the other. It sent a prickling heat straight down to her clit, which throbbed impatiently once again for his attention.

He flung off his jacket then fumbled about and found the side zipper to her dress. In marathon speed, he had the clingy material pooling at her ankles. The delicate lace thong soon followed, leaving her completely naked to his appreciating gaze. Pressing her flush against his body, two fingers pushed inside her pussy as his thumb concentrated on that pulsating nerve, working her jerky body until she said his name on a low throaty cry, gripping his shoulders tight, trembling and splintering into thousands of incredible pieces. His arm around her waist was what kept her upright before he scooped her up and carried her to his bed. He flicked on the bedside lamp. Its dim wattage cast him in beautiful shadows. She lay upon his cool sheets in a sensory fog, watching him stripped down to golden-brown flesh, his shade like that of sweet, warm pecan candy. She moistened her lips with deeply savored anticipation.

He took a condom from his wallet, tore into the black wrapper with his teeth, and rolled the thin latex down that massive part of him, its bulbous head wet and ready.

She laughed at the feel of his tongue and warm breath

brushing across her toes. His hands skated up her legs, fingers kneading her calves, adding just the right pressure along the way before he kissed her behind the knee and nipped her there, continuing a warm brush of his lips slowly upward. He paused and reared back, studying her tattoo that rode the right side curve of of her pelvis. His eyes came up.

"This wasn't here before."

"Kennedi, Tabitha, and I have the same design. It's a sistahood thing. A story for another day."

A smiled formed. "I like it."

Light kisses followed the leafy ivy vine down to the vee of her mound, his tongue paying extra attention at the split of her folds. She nearly bucked off the bed, her hands squeezing the sheet with each long, deliberate sweep at her swollen nub.

When he'd tortured her clit beyond reason, he came up over her and licked an exquisite trail up the offering angle of her throat, reaccelerating that astounding buzz of need that simmered just below an overboil within. She clasped hold of his face with both hands and sealed her mouth to his, her tongue snaking within, taking what she wanted with a demanding urgency that he'd encouraged all the way up from her toes.

With his gaze fixed on hers, he slipped a hand between them, pressed his penis at her opening, and entered her fully, completely. She closed her eyes on a wild shudder as it all came rushing back—their scorching remembered union of body and soul. What followed was nothing but sensation, the hot, huge glide of his thick hard shaft stroking deep within her wet walls.

She ran her hands over bulky wide shoulders, lean back, and firm ass, refamiliarizing herself with his spectacular landscape before she nudged him to roll over and straddled his hips. His stare never fluttered, locked tight with hers as she took her pleasure, riding wildly, holding nothing back.

"Vinny," she breathed.

He blinked, eyes glowing hot in the dim light, sat up, and clamped on to her buttocks, driving her to grind down on his length, igniting a hot-edged friction that left them both panting ferociously. On a quick flip, he pressed her into the mattress, his hips working with maddening speed as his kisses maintained a greedy insistence.

The tide swelled, overtaking them. Her ankles locked at his back as a fierce tightening shot through her sex, her channel clamping down hard at the feel of him pulsing high up inside her. With a final, glorious shudder, he collapsed on top of her, their sweaty, heaving bodies jerking through small aftershocks. When she was able to regain control of her limbs, she stroked the broad expanse of his back, enjoying the full weight of his satiated body crushing hers.

It'd been so long since she'd felt so completely quenched. He was the embodiment of pleasure. It was everything she remembered, as though there hadn't been twelve years of lost time between them. "That was…amazing!"

He came up on his elbows and helped himself to the taste of her tongue, devouring her mouth, easily overwhelming her senses, then reared back. Gentle fingertips skated along her cheek. "It was as wonderful as it always was with you."

Evie felt him slipping free of her body, but she didn't

want to break the warm connection. Reluctantly, she unwrapped herself from around him. He got up and crossed to the bathroom. She took the short minutes to straighten the rumpled sheets and grab the light blanket that had found its way to the floor during their lovemaking.

Lovemaking. Before she could mull over that one word that had her heart on a major pitter-patter, he returned to the bed and clicked off the lamp. She curled into the cocoon of his big body, spooning in tight within his comforting warmth while suddenly wondering if she was the center of his world for tonight only. Were there others? A budding irritation stirred at the thought. Was she so shallow to think he didn't have other lovers? He was indeed a magnificent catch. She didn't have the right to be annoyed nor a right for him to be solely hers.

But the rational conclusion didn't stop her from wanting it. Though it all gnawed at her, she closed her eyes and let the pulse of his heavy breathing carry her off to sleep.

Chapter Fourteen

V INCENT'S INTERNAL CLOCK woke him, still on East Coast time. The bright red digital numbers on the nightstand, the only illumination in the otherwise dark space, showed 5:07 a.m.

He turned his head and smiled, enjoying the light rumble of Evie's slumber. *And she claims I snore.*

Her warm palm rested on his chest. A smooth calf lay across his shin. He carefully reached over, trying his best not to disturb her, and turned on the lamp but kept the bulb at a soft glow, just enough to take in the beautiful, naked woman beside him.

She was stretched out on her stomach, practically in the center of the bed. Hogging the mattress was something he recalled she tended to do. She'd kicked the covers off them both—another of her familiar sleeping habits.

The joy and contentment to just listen to her expel the subtle puffs of air was indescribable. Waking up to her like this, to her in his bed, to her refilling that hollow space in his chest that he'd boarded up tight because of her, it shook him up with all sorts of complex emotions. But, damn, how he wanted her. Physically, yes, but he craved so much more. Could they start over?

Then, there was her ex. William Drexel's call yesterday to report his findings on Patrick had been interesting but not surprising. It was what had been unearthed about Evie's family that had shocked Vincent speechless. He was unable to get the full breakdown. More detail was needed before he said anything to Evie.

He eased himself free of her limbs and slipped on his boxers. She stirred, rolling over. The stiff points of her nipples begged to be kissed. On a resigned sigh, he fought the nearly impossible temptation and left the bed.

When her soft, even breathing resumed, he padded out, and carefully closed the door.

His jacket, her dress, purse, and shoes lay in a heap at the entry door, reminded of the wild high level of passion that took hold of them last night. He gathered up everything and retrieved his phone from the inside pocket to call Will. The line connected almost instantly.

"Vincent, good morning."

He moved to the kitchen area and tried to keep his voice low. "Morning, Will. Plans changed last night. I'm still in Vegas. I didn't want to wait until I got back to talk. You said Patrick is a partner on the vineyard abroad, not just his parents?"

"That's correct. Reese's report shows him as majority owner."

The asset hadn't been listed as part of the settlement. That asshole was trying to keep Evie from getting her share. "About that other matter, are you absolutely certain what you told me is accurate?" It was a ridiculous question. Will didn't fuck around. Former military special ops turned private security entrepreneur, William Drexel did his homework thoroughly. And he had a team carrying those same credentials. But the information the investigation revealed about Evie was so astonishing, Vincent couldn't wrap his head around it.

"You said Evie's adopted mother is in fact her birth mother? How can that be?"

"Between my team and I, we found evidence that shows Charlotte Bennett married at age twenty to Henry Langston, age twenty-five. Evie was born a little over a year later."

"I know the story. When Evie and I met, she told me about her birth mother, Sonya Johnson, who died when Evie was four. Sonya and Charlotte were best friends. Evie went to live with Charlotte and Henry and was officially adopted at age nine."

"That may have been what Evie was told. The records and information we found tell a different story. At age twenty-one, Charlotte gave birth to a daughter in a hospital down in Durham, S.C. Sonya lived in Durham. According to documents, Charlotte's place of residence was New York. I can only assume she handed Evie over to her friend, Sonya, soon after she was born. But Sonya then moved to New York as well. Info also shows Charlotte was enrolled in grad school at Brown during this time."

"If Evie's biracial and Charlotte's her biological mother, that rules out Henry Langston."

"Yes. I called in a favor to a buddy of mine who's active duty and has accesses. He supplied me a complete timeline of Langston's service record. Within the window Evie would've been conceived and Charlotte giving birth, Henry Langston was stationed overseas. By the time he returned stateside, Evie was three. Sonya died a year later. The rest of the story lines up with what Evie knows today."

"Damn." Vincent rubbed a rough hand back and forth over the top of his head. What should he do with this web of information?

"Vincent, man, I've done this job long enough and have seen a lot. I didn't think anything could raise my eyebrows until this. To the point—"

"Charlotte had an affair while her husband was actively serving overseas." Vincent supplied what had become obvious.

"Yes, I'm afraid that's the way the pieces are fitting to-gether. With her friend Sonya's help, she hid the baby from her husband. I guess she didn't count on Sonya being diagnosed and succumbing to leukemia. Given that Evie still believes she's adopted, it's likely Henry is in the dark about it."

Retired army colonel turned IT professional, a mother with a master's in psychology from Brown University, an overachieving daughter, and a son who graduated from the Naval Academy, the Langstons were the picture-perfect American family unit. If Henry somehow discovered his wife held such a shady secret from him, but didn't call her out on it, he was extremely forgiving and a damn saint.

"Did you find out anything about the biological father?"

"As a matter fact, yes. An African American man named Julius Mitchell. Charlotte and Julius attended the same high school. Captain of the varsity football team. Decent grades, but nowhere near Ivy League. Yearbook photos I've obtained show quite a few events where Julius and Charlotte were together. Sad to say, he was among the first killed in the Gulf War."

"There you are."

Vincent turned to Evie standing behind him wrapped in the bedsheet. Soft green eyes tranquil from sleep; dark-toffee tresses appeared arranged by the comb-through of fingers. Damn, how sexy. He yearned to wake each day to her looking just like this. "Will, I'll catch up with you later. Thanks for the quick turnaround."

"I'll get the hard copy data over to you. If you need anything else, you know where to find me."

They disconnected. "Hey. Hope I didn't wake you."

"I rolled over and you weren't there. Did I push you out of the bed? You used to claim I kickbox in my sleep."

"Oh, you still do." Her amusement told him she hadn't caught any of his conversation with Will. "I had some digging done on Patrick and discovered he's majority owner of his parents' vineyard abroad. He didn't list it among the assets. You're entitled to half of his percentage. Did you know he held that level of ownership?"

"No, but if it means him not getting a portion of the bakery, he can keep his vineyard."

"You'll be relinquishing a substantial amount of money. The wine is distributed around the globe."

"I don't want the money or anything to do with it. I'm fine with my share of the bakery. It's enough for me."

"Evie, give it some thought."

"Vincent, I'm okay." She smiled. "I don't need much."

And just like that, the conflict he'd had with their past

and present fell away. "Expect to have papers to sign this week."

"That's wonderful. I've been concerned that Patrick would try to drag things out like he has been."

"I won't let that happen."

"I didn't mean to disturb your call. Oh, that reminds me." She whirled around. "I need to text Tab and Kenni. Have you seen my purse?"

Vincent pointed to the center table over in the living room.

"Goodness. My phone was blowing up last night. I have about ten text messages. A few also from my mom. She's going to kill me if I don't get caught up on the next two episodes of *S.W.A.T.*"

He didn't know how to tell her about her mother. The information was so damn heavy.

Dawn crept in through the wall of glass, stamping out shadows. Time. He needed a barrel of it. "I thought we'd complete the weekend in Vegas, if you're up for it."

"I don't have anything to wear."

"It's Vegas. Boutiques will come to you."

"Well, in that case, I'm up for it. But first." She came forward, hips swaying, a seductive smile playing about her lips, and spread the sheet open wide, revealing her hot, nude body. "Come back to bed."

He nodded, grinning. "I can do that."

Chapter Fifteen

"FELLAS, WHAT DO you think I should do?" Seated at Blacksalt's crowded seafood market restaurant, Vincent searched his buddies across the table for advice. He'd just shared with them what he'd discovered about Evie's parentage.

"You should tell her," Trenton advised.

"No." Dominic shook his head as he worked down the last hefty portion of his fish taco and took a long pull of his soda through the straw. "Don't say a damn thing to her about it. Learning that your adopted mother is your birth mother—that fact alone would land me on a shrink's couch for years. Add to it, your mother gave you over to her best friend to raise only so she could hide her infidelity from her husband. And don't forget the trauma she must have gone through as a child when the woman she thought was her mother—" air quotes "—passed away."

Trenton sat back, expelling a breath. "Damn, when you put it like that, it makes it hard for me not to agree." He looked over at Vincent. "Bro, you and Evie just spent the weekend together. The revelation about her mother could potentially affect anything that could grow from that. I hate to say it. Whichever direction you take, you might end up on the losing end."

That was the core of where his problem resided.

Vincent pushed his untouched blue-crabcake sandwich away, no longer having an appetite. His hollow stomach churned and turned over. He knew what he needed to do.

"HELLO, EVERYONE," EVIE cheerfully greeted Chase Confections's busy kitchen staff.

Kennedi turned. "Look who decided to join us on this fine Monday…" Smiling, she glanced up to the clock stationed above the door. "Afternoon."

"And she appears quite gleeful, if I do say so." Tabitha rested back against the counter, arms folded, a cheeky grin dotting her lips. "How was your weekend? Do I dare ask?"

"Good." Evie signaled with a side-nod toward the custom cake room. Her red canvas Chucks did feel featherlight on her feet as she sauntered over and closed the door after they crossed the threshold. "Sorry for being late. I know we have a packed schedule. How were things around here over the weekend? No issues, I hope." Both stared back at her. "What?"

"Sista-girl, don't play." Tabitha gave her a lighthearted shove. "Vincent whisked you off to Vegas for dinner on Friday and you show up Monday afternoon smiling and bopping about with twinkling stars in your eyes. We're going to need a lot more than *good*."

"Yes, get to spilling," Kennedi added, and they both sat on the edge of the desk with wide smiles.

Evie was upbeat and blissfully wrapped tight in a twine of plain old joy. A good bit of the past three days was spent in Vincent's strong, wonderful arms. Deliciously trapped beneath his muscle-cut limbs. Straddled atop his magnificently hard thighs. "It was amazing!" she burst, practically giddy. "I think I had more sex in three days than my entire seven years of marriage. I know Vincent and I were together before and all, but my goodness, it was..." she stared heavenward, reminded of the sensual high that still hadn't completely subsided "...explosive." She beamed, unable to stop smiling. It'd been so long since she'd been so freaking happy.

"You go, girl!" Kennedi cheered.

"It's like riding a bike." Tabitha grinned.

Over the years, Evie had shared her woes about Patrick's activities in the bedroom...or, more to the point, his lack thereof.

"It was an amazing weekend, but I don't see anything moving forward while Vincent's working on my case. That said, I should have my divorce papers soon. I won't have to give up any portion of my percentage of Chase Confections. He took care of that, too."

"That's wonderful," Kennedi said, and she and Tabitha hugged her.

Evie's chest swelled with immeasurable affection for Vincent even as her heart grew a bit heavy with regret. "Twelve years we wasted being apart. I often wonder where he and I would be today had I not said those things I did. If only I hadn't pressured him about school or listened to my mom. I was a snob. I didn't deserve him." Her eyes watered and easily spilled over. Both ladies hurriedly tucked her close within their supportive embrace. "We would've been happy had I appreciated the wonderful man he is."

"Don't beat yourself up." Tabitha swiped away the tear on Evie's cheek with her thumb. "You guys found your way back to each other. That's what matters."

"Tab's right. Leave the past where it is. Concentrate on the now, starting with…" Kennedi grabbed the schedule log from the desk along with the design sketches, divvying up the jobs among them. "We have a total of five projects going out this week."

On Evie's plate was an eight-year-old's birthday racecar and the graduation cake for Sasha.

Tabitha turned on the music, then each moved to a metal tabletop with their designs in hand, jumping right in.

Evie exhaled deep, expelling the past with it, and looked forward to her future, confident it included Vincent.

Over the next several hours, she fell into a steady groove. Carlos, as well as Patrice, their junior pastry chefs, and even Tabitha's apprentice, Brielle, assisted each of them where needed. By the time Evie looked up at the clock, it was closing in on eight thirty. It was just her and Kennedi now, who held a deep concentration, shaping the gum paste for the roof on the castle. She was a master at creating elaborate structures.

"Hey, you need any help?"

"I think I got it." Kennedi looked up. "Go home. Get some rest."

"You're sure?"

"Yes, I'm good."

"Okay. I'll see you in the morning."

Evie said a few words to the kitchen staff, then headed out front. The bakery closed in about an hour, yet there were a decent number of tables occupied. "Amy, I can hang around if you need an extra hand."

"No, I got it covered. We're fully staffed tonight. Besides, I'm sure your friend is probably tired of waiting."

Evie frowned. "My friend?"

"The one who came before." Amy angled her head to the side. "That guy over there. He's been here about an hour or so."

They peered across the room to where Vincent sat at a café table near the right corner end of the storefront window. His tie hung loosely knotted around the collar of his pale blue button-down, the sleeves rolled up the forearms. With his phone pinned to his ear, he scribbled away on a notepad.

"Why didn't you tell me?"

"He said you knew he was here and to let you work, not to disturb you. I offered him something to eat on the house, but he declined."

She watched Vincent rest the pen on the table and pinch his eyes before rolling his neck and shoulders. The ballpoint was quickly back in his hand, scribbling away. His presence was a pleasant surprise after a long day.

"Should I have let you know he was here?" Amy asked.

"No. I, uh, it's fine."

Amy elbowed her, smiling. "That serious look on his face, he's just the right amount of rugged drizzled over a whole lotta cute."

Evie chuckled. "I won't even ask what that means. You

have a good night." She made her way to Vincent's table. "Hey."

His attention came up from his notepad, his expression set into that all-business, don't bother me mood while he continued his dialogue about some sort of legal matter. Then, a pressed-lipped smile spread up into his cheeks, softening his broodily handsome face as he hung up, closed his portfolio, and came to his feet. "Evening. Thought I'd come by to drive you home."

"You didn't have to do that."

"Probably not smart of me." He glanced out at the night through the window where the hustle and bustle of pedestrians never seemed to wane. "But you won't get a car, so you leave me little choice." He ushered her out the door. "I'm just down the block."

"I don't need a car. Look." She gave a wave at the line of Uber and Lyft drivers on constant rotation. The cars were getting picked off about as fast as their passengers exited the back seat. "As you know my commute really isn't very far."

They made the short walk and got into his car. Before she realized what was happening, he hooked a hand at the back of her neck and pulled her into the hungry crush of his mouth, stealing her breath. She poured herself into the warmth of his kiss, swirling her tongue with his, holding nothing back until they were both winded.

As his gaze held hers, a gentle palm cupped her cheek, his thumb stroking. "You know I care about you, right?" he voiced softly. "Don't forget that."

She nodded, regarding the seriousness on his face, but told herself not to make more out of it.

His mouth descended on hers once more, kissing her slow and easy, the feel of his smooth lips soothing better than any balm ever could. When he finally drew back, the warmth reflecting in his eyes made her heart kick up and spread heat in her veins like flames within dried brush.

"I'll be heading tomorrow to New York with Trent for a meeting with his investors. I should be back late Friday."

"Just in time for the party."

"Yeah, don't remind me." He reached to the back seat. "I have your papers."

Evie gaped. "They're done already?" She took the weighty, legal-sized envelope. "This is great."

"I didn't want to give the opposing counsel any time to try to change the verbally agreed-upon terms."

"Yes, well, I wouldn't put anything past Patrick. He'd do it purely out of spite."

"Hence." He angled his head at the document on her lap that would finally undo the shackles to Patrick's twisted control and held the key to her future with the man seated beside her.

"Before you sign, you should really consider taking your portion of his assets. In addition to the vineyard, he has other private accounts abroad as well. I'm talking substantial amounts. And you weren't aware of any of it?" he asked while pulling into the flow of traffic and zipping the car out of the city.

"Well, I thought the vineyard was his parents'. I didn't know he had a large stake in it."

"It's more his than theirs. No doubt it's why he agreed to give up his portion of the bakery so readily and accepted your terms of no alimony. On that note, you'll find two versions in the envelope. The red-tabbed document spells out your counteroffer, which includes you getting your entitled percentage of his holdings. The other document tabbed in green is your agreed-upon terms as they stand. Copies of his investments and statements are there in the package. Review everything before you sign away your rights if you so choose to go that direction."

"I can imagine what you must think of me." When no reply came, she stared straight ahead, feeling equal parts stunned and foolish for allowing herself to be so gullible. The fact stung her like a hard slap to the face. But wasn't that part of what a marriage, a partnership between two people meant? Trust without suspicion? She directed her focus out her window at the whizzing Beltway traffic, hiding the hurt and angry tears brimming in her eyes. Her deceitful ex didn't warrant the pain of betrayal stabbing her heart.

Warm fingers laced with hers. "He's an asshole and didn't deserve you." Vincent pressed a tender kiss to her knuckles, providing that small, much-needed lifeline, dousing her melancholy mood.

The Tesla rolled through her parted gates, and—as was his custom—he assisted her out of the car. She wrapped her arms around his neck, yearning to touch him, be held by him, and gave him a tender peck on the lips. "Thank you, of course, for the ride, and for everything else."

"No need to thank me. We had a deal, remember?" He cut a small smile, but it didn't quite reach his weary eyes. On a deep breath in and slow release, he looked away a moment then back at her, his features returning to all severe angles as he reached up and peeled her arms away but held on to both hands.

"Can we talk?"

The solemn way those three words breached his lips raised the hairs on her arms. *We're moving too fast. Been there with you, done that. Let's be friends with benefits.* But what about his sweet greeting kiss? *I care about you*, he'd said. A thousand mixed meanings raced through her head. Her heart was suddenly pounding.

"Okay. Sure." They took the stairs up and into the house. Evie used her phone to disarm the alarm, then dropped her satchel onto the entry table. With her fingers curled around his, she led them upstairs, into her bedroom. "You're all tense." She unknotted his tie the rest of the way and slipped it off, followed by the release of button after button, down to where the shirt disappeared within the waistband of his slacks. She tugged loose his belt and brought down the zipper, then stepped back. "I think you need a massage." She wanted to distract and prolong what might be coming as she toed out of her sneakers and stripped down to bare skin.

A breath left him; the intensity of his heavy-lidded gaze roamed over her. "You have to be naked to give me a massage? I thought we were going to talk."

"We will." She guided him to sit on the cushioned bench at the foot of the bed, kneeled, and unbuckled his shoes, forcing his shiny wingtips and socks off his size fourteen feet. He stood and dragged down his pants and boxers. She took him by the hand again and led the way into the doorless shower, its steam almost instantly fogging the mirrors. As he stood beneath the spray, she chose among the essential oils sitting within the wall niche and filled her palm.

"What's that?" He took the bottle and sniffed. "You're going to have me smelling like you."

"It's valerian, lavender, and vetiver. I call it nature's tranquil trio. The combination will help you relax." She started in on the tightness in his neck, catching pulse points, then worked the knots in his back and shoulders, concentrating for long seconds in some areas that felt like hard stone beneath smooth skin. As she worked her thumbs down his spine, adding pressure, he closed his eyes on a heavy sigh, head low, and braced a hand upon the wet tile. When she kneaded his firm ass, a deep-chested rumble expelled from him.

"Feels good, right?"

"Damn, you have no idea."

She bent, continuing her ministrations along the muscles of his thick thighs and solid calves, taking her time to stroked away the stiffness, then came to her feet and grabbed the most mildly scented shower gel she had. He took it from her, quickly washed himself, then rinsed. Before she knew it, he was running his soapy hands all over her body.

"It's just what you needed to take away the stress," she said as the warm water slid down her frame.

He caught her at the waist, jerking her against his hot, wet skin, and captured her mouth in a searing kiss. "You're what I need." Light fingers slid between her legs and stroked her sex with maddening slowness. Two fingers invaded her pussy, leisurely thrusting, in and out. The other hand splayed across her buttocks, drawing her even closer as their tongues dueled sweetly. She clung to his slick, hard shoulders, her desire revving, demanding to be slaked, while her mind fell into a state of calm. She was wrong about him wanting to cut things off. At least not behind closed doors.

It occurred to her. She knew it bothered him that she didn't wish to pursue her entitled percentage of her ex's assets. He was going to try to convince her to sign the red-tabbed document.

He shut off the faucet, then started walking her backward out of the shower, tracking wet feet toward the door.

She doubled back and grabbed bath towels, quickly buffing off before he took her hand and ushered to her bed, both sliding between cool linens. His head ducked underneath. His wide shoulders settled between her spread thighs. His mouth clamped on to her sex, and for long, glorious minutes, he licked and tongued her with a nonstop rhythm. Panting, she fisted the sheet as her body fell into a savage state of ecstasy, the pleasure climbing so high, she saw stars bursting behind her closed lids.

She rocked her hips swiftly on his wonderfully working mouth, catching, holding him at the back of his head to keep him just where she needed until the damn broke, her back arching and legs trembling as he sent her into a mind-spiraling orgasm.

He crawled torturously slow up her body, kissing her hot skin along the way. His teeth grazed and caught her sensitive nipple. The aggressive tugging and light swirls of his tongue, from one to the other, a wild combination of sharp and gentle, sent shivers throughout her body before he finally claimed her mouth, stealing her breath. Her heart was banging against her breastbone by the time he eased up and braced himself upon his elbows above her.

"Vinny, what you do to me," she breathed, taking in much-needed air. He was such a magnificent lover. "I felt that literally all the way from my toes."

He grinned quite cheekily. "A little payback for the naked, wet massage." As the tips of his fingers trailed the outline of her jaw, that look of disquiet returned to his face. "Evie, I was young and stupid. So many times, after we had that big fight, I wanted to reach out to you to say I'm sorry. Instead, I let my stubbornness and need to be right strip me of twelve years with you."

"Vincent—" He silenced her with a touch of his lips to hers.

"What I'm trying to say is I never stopped loving you."

Evie gasped, heart pounding.

"I know that might be a lot to take in, but I needed to say it."

His eyes held hers, sincere and tender, leaving her once again without words. She cupped his face in both hands and pulled him down to her mouth, gentle at first, then slid quickly into full-on passion. A subtle sound rumbled up from his chest, a clear sign of surrender as his hand slid between their bodies. The head of his penis breached her opening, but she caught his wrist.

"We need a condom."

He blinked, then nodded. Though it wasn't necessary, she explained, "I'm not on any contraceptive, not yet. I haven't been sexually active since my separation."

"I understand." He lifted off her.

"Wait." She remembered the condoms Tabitha had given her. "I'll be right back." She dashed into her closet then climbed back in bed with the small black box. "I have these. Tab got them for me after you and me… We…"

His right eyebrow raised, lips quirking. "Magnum XL?"

She blushed. "It was a good, educated guess."

He snagged a quick peck on her lips, then ripped opened the packaging and tore into the gold wrapper. The thin latex hugged snugly along his thick shaft.

When their bodies joined, fitting together perfectly, she kept pace with the power of his deep thrusts, and called his name repeatedly on a primal wail of rapture. His hands latched on to her buttocks, squeezing as his hips surged, practically fucking her into the mattress.

With swift movements, he repositioned himself behind her, their bodies spooning. His hand wedged beneath her and captured a breast. The other caught her leg at the back of the knee, anchoring her pose before he entered her sex from the rear. Determined fingers found her clit, and for long minutes, he worked the sensitive nerve, keeping pace with his rapid surges.

The pleasure was so intense, a spectacular prism of ecstasy, the tide washed over her in a wild rush of shivers. On his last harsh plunge, his body became a taut column throughout the spasms striking deep inside her. He tucked his head at the back of her neck, breath sawing in and out like an overrun motor. Then, he tilted her head back with a light nudge at her chin and trekked a series of hot licks along her throat to her offering mouth, kissing her as if still unquenched by the blistering unleashing of his passions.

He rolled on to his back, chest heaving, breath choppy.

She did the same, her breathing just as labored—their skin damp—their needs thoroughly slaked, fiercely, sweetly.

Their heads turned, facing one another, and both smiled before he left the bed.

Evie scooted over, smoothing the covers, feeling immensely content. When he returned, she eagerly tucked herself in close within the warmth of his body, enjoying the not-so-even pumps of his heartbeat against her ear. They relaxed quietly in a comfortable sprawl of twined limbs.

"You said you wanted to talk."

"Um-hum."

"I'm listening." All she heard was the thump of his pulse having found its natural beat. She smiled. He'd apparently succumbed to the full weight of his exhaustion. Within short minutes, her eyes closed, easily joining him.

THE WELCOMING AROMA of rich, roasted chicory woke Vincent from a sound, restful sleep. He turned over on buttery-soft cotton sheets, intent on waking Evie with the brush of a kiss, followed by a repeat of their passionate lovemaking shared the night before, only to make contact with cool, empty space. The bathroom door was open across the room; no sound was heard. Within a wall niche, a Keurig streamed coffee into a carafe. *Cool.* It must have been on a timer. High vaulted ceiling skylights offered windows to view a cloudless, clear morning. Sunlight filtered through white sheer curtains, brushing over plush upholstery done in pale yellows and soft grays.

But he felt an undercurrent of saltiness. To be in the room, in the bed, where Evie held shared memories with that asshat of a husband… The thought sent Vincent upright, but it was the sight of the note atop the legal docs littered with his green tabs on the nightstand that coaxed him to rational reason. He flipped to the signature pages where she'd inked her legal name, then read her note.

> *I had to get to work early.*
>
> *You probably wanted to talk about pursuing my half of Patrick's holdings. It would only prolong ties with him. I want to close that chapter of my life so I can concentrate on building my future with you.*
>
> *The entry door will lock automatically when you close it.*
>
> *Have a safe trip to New York.*
>
> *-E*

He regarded the two twined hearts she'd drawn next to her initial.

Yes, he wanted to touch on her getting a cut of Patrick's assets, but it took a back seat to what really needed to be laid bare.

He got dressed, made his way downstairs and out the front door, hoping that by telling Evie how he felt about her, she'd draw on that when he turned her world upside down.

Chapter Sixteen

Evie glanced up from her project to Tabitha entering the cake room. "Hey."

"Good morning." Tabitha shot a frown at the TV screen. "What, no music today? We're watching shows now while we work?" She grabbed her apron from the wall hook and came forward. "I need beats to get the day's adrenaline flowing."

"It's almost over." Evie carefully set the racecar's left rear tire into place. "There." She straightened and rolled her neck, stretching out the kinks. "I'm watching the next episode with my mom later. She likes to recap. I couldn't watch last night. Vincent stayed over." She smirked.

"Nice." Tabitha grinned.

"Morning, ladies." Kennedi entered the room and snagged an apron. "Wow, that car is turning out great. It's almost done. When did you get here?"

"Around six."

"Vincent stayed over last night." Tabitha winked.

Kennedi's grin spread wide. "Did he now? I guess things are going well."

Evie's impish smile matched theirs. "Very well. I signed my divorce papers." They shrieked and smothered her with hugs. "We—"

"Excuse me." Amy entered. "Evie, oh my goodness, you have to come see this. The guy who gave me this to give to you said he left the car parked in the reserved spot out front."

Evie was handed a small envelope with no markings. She opened it to find a note along with a key, the GM emblem inscribed in the metal. She unfolded the paper and read:

Since you won't get your own, you can use mine.

Take care of my baby. See you Friday.

Miss you already.

"Who gave you this?" Evie asked Amy.

"He said his name was Mac. He asked to speak to the supervisor. I told him that was me, then he only said to give that to you. He seemed in a hurry."

"What car?" Tabitha asked.

"Come see."

Evie snapped off her gloves, and they followed Amy out of the store to the curb, where a shiny black classic Chevy Camaro convertible sat, its crisp white leather interior and spotless chrome finishes basking in the morning sunrays. Orange caution cones were strategically stationed at the front and rear bumpers, defining the distance for anyone who would even think of parking too close. She stared, stunned. "No way! It can't be."

"Wow, that's boss," Amy remarked before retreating inside.

"It's Vincent's, I take it," Kennedi said.

Evie nodded, near speechless. "It's the '69 model. I was there when he bought the rusted-out piece of junk. He swore it was a diamond in the rough, insisted that I try to look beyond the ugly to see the jewel underneath. Rally wheels, rear spoiler, dual exhaust—it's all what he said he'd someday do to it. We argued for days about it." Her eyes glistened; a tear moistened her cheek. "I called him foolish for spending a thousand dollars on it, which was steep for him back then. I was the fool. I should've had more faith in him."

Kennedi took her hand. "It's okay."

"Anyone who can restore a vintage whip to look this good has serious skills." Tabitha circled the vehicle. "It doesn't have a scratch on it." She looked at Evie and smiled. "Be very careful."

Evie shook her head. "I can't drive it."

"Nonsense. Things are good with you two. Can you just let yourself be happy? No more tears, understand?" Tabitha delivered a stern stare, yet tender thumbs swept across Evie's damp cheeks. "Now, let's get some work done."

Kennedi pulled open the door.

"I'll be there in a minute." When they disappeared inside, Evie retrieved her phone from her back pocket, dialed with anxious anticipation to hear his voice. A few rings, then the line connected.

"Good morning, beautiful."

"I love you, Vincent…"

"Dude, are you on your way?"

"I'm pulling in now," Vincent answered Trenton and disconnected the call as he parked the Tesla in the airplane's hangar. With his garment bag and carry-on in tow, he jogged up the airstairs and entered the cabin. "Sorry, fellas, for holding you up. I had to rush home to shower and take care of a few things," he said to Trenton and Dominic, who was stuffing his face with a plate of pancakes and sausage.

"For a minute there, I thought you opted to fly commercial." Dominic shuddered.

Vincent chuckled and plopped down on the couch. "Your ass is spoiled." Spence entered the cabin rolling a cart that carried a carafe of much-needed coffee. "My man, you read my mind."

"Good morning, Mr. Scott. Would you like some breakfast?" He handed off a steaming cup of the rich, black pick-me-up before putting away the luggage.

"No, thanks. This right here is all I need." Vincent took a good swallow and relaxed against the thick leather cushions, disregarding the two sets of blue eyes pinned on him. "Trent, I have the docs ready for you to sign."

"What was that about needing to rush home to shower?" Trenton asked once Spence vacated.

"Yeah, don't think we didn't pick up on that little slide-in info. Hmm, let's see." Dominic scratched his chin. "You fell into a sewage well on the way here and needed a shower. You got doused with bird shit and needed a shower." He laughingly poked with a wave of his fork. "I'm afraid we're going to need you to elaborate."

"Like Dom said, it could be any number of reasons you needed to rush home this morning." Trenton grinned, tag-teaming with his brother.

Vincent had been friends with the pair since about

twelve years old. A chance meeting in Scout camp had led to a lifelong brotherhood. "You two are dicks, you know that, right?" He shook his head at their rather proud, shared hard nods.

"But seriously, bro, did you tell Evie about that situation with her mother?" Trenton asked.

"I haven't told her."

"I still don't think you should tell her, but if she discovers that you knew and didn't tell her, I can't see that going over well," Dominic said.

"He's got a point," Trenton remarked. "What will you do?"

Vincent's cell phone ring saved him from answering. The sight of Evie calling made his pulse do a strange fluttering flip, and he was completely aware what it meant. He'd lived in this poignant space with her before. Hell, his feelings had never left; they'd sat dormant beneath the veil of hurt, only to bloom even stronger than before.

He opened the line. "Good morning, beautiful."

"I love you, Vincent. I signed the document with the green tabs instead of the red to get it over and done with. I want to start my life with you. I've lost twelve years without you. I don't want to miss another single day."

Vincent blinked, his chest jackhammering. There it was, on display in its raw emotional form. Smiling, unable to suppress the feeling, he got up and went into the sleeping cabin at the back of the plane for a bit of privacy. "That's good to hear. Really good." His heart swelled to near pain, as if trying to burst through his rib cage. "I want that too. I'll have the papers fully executed and filed."

"I also have the car. It's parked, but I'm sitting in the driver's seat right now. A 1969 Chevrolet Camaro—it's the one you purchased from that junkyard…I-I mean the place with the old cars. Vin, it's so beautiful, I'm afraid to even turn on the radio. You fully restored it just as you said you would."

"It took about five years, but yes. I drive it now and then to flush the motor, but it mostly sits covered in my garage. Thought you could use it this week while I'm away."

"Thank you. I'll be careful."

"I know you will. There's something I've kept in the glove box that belongs to you. Take a look." He heard a distinct gasp.

"My infinity pink pearl bracelet. You still have it."

"I'd saved for months, worked overtime to get you that."

"I remember."

"I had to keep it. Besides, it did leave a knot in the center of my forehead for days when you threw it at me. You had great aim and a solid arm, by the way." He laughed, then tensed at the sudden weeping sound. "It was a joke. Evie? Baby? I deserved the lick I got." *Shit, what have I done?* "Please don't cry." He wanted to be there to hold her. The tone of her sadness pounded at the center of his chest.

"Vincent, I'm sorry for all the things I said and did." Still, her cries cut through her wobbly voice.

"We both said things that were hurtful. And that's okay. Just know I love you, all right?" Her sorrow eased to soft sniffles. "I'll be back Friday and will miss you until then. I love you."

"I love you."

He returned to the main cabin, took a seat, and let out a harsh breath while wanting to kick his own ass.

"You're good," Trenton asked.

"Yeah."

I'm beyond screwed.

Chapter Seventeen

EVIE GRABBED HER glasses from the nightstand, climbed in bed, and turned on the TV before bringing up the video chat on her computer. Her mom's face appeared almost instantly, wearing her usual bright-pink-cheek smile. Her shoulder-length, golden-blonde hair pulled back into a ponytail seemingly added a bit of lift to her narrow jaw and brought out a youthfulness in her pretty features. Family and friends often said Evie's and her mom's eyes were similar in shape. Of course, it was impossible, but the bond with her mom was so tightly woven, she liked to pretend it was so.

"Hi, sweetheart. Tonight's going to be really good. Are you caught up?"

"I am." *Sort of.* She'd glanced at the TV only during action-packed points while working.

"Great. The last episode was a cliffhanger."

They always allowed a few minutes to recap. "Mom, I'm seeing someone," Evie blurted, using the time to spring the news. Her mom's cheerful gray eyes jumped wide.

"Oh! Okay. Well, tell me about him. Is he as handsome as Shemar Moore?" she asked with a taunt of a grin.

"Actually, uh, it's Vincent Scott."

"Vincent?" Her brow furrowed. "The guy you were seeing when you were in college? The mechanic?"

Evie didn't correct her. "We're dating again. He lives here in D.C. now." Her mom's tight features said more than any words would have. The disapproving silence was deafening. She sighed, expelling the tension with it. "Mom, just say what I know you want to say. You didn't hide your feelings about him when we dated before, so you may as well not do it now."

"That's because he wasn't doing anything with his life. He dropped out of college to become a mechanic, for goodness' sake. Who does that?"

"He was…is a damn good mechanic!" Evie snapped. "There's nothing wrong with that. Had I realized it back then, we might have stayed together, maybe even gotten married like he wanted. But instead, I let you get into my head. And what did I end up with? A verbally abusive, controlling husband who felt he owned my very soul."

"Evie, I wish you'd told me." Her voice grew tender. "Honey, all I'm saying is getting your divorce is an opportunity to explore your options."

"I've already found the man for me. I love him. You can accept him for the magnificent man he is, or don't. Either way, this time, I'm not letting him get away." Her mom's laser stare worked up a stockpile of insecurities. Evie couldn't recall ever speaking to her that way.

"You're an adult and can make your own decisions." Awkward was the atmosphere around the sip of her tea. "We've missed the show's opening."

She gave a glance at her TV, her mood low. "I'm going to turn in. I have to be at the store by six tomorrow morning."

"Oh." Eyelids fluttered. Her mom looked away, but not before the gleam of hurt reflected in her gaze. "Sleep well."

"Good night."

The video screen went black. Evie turned off the TV, shut her laptop, and slid down beneath the covers, making herself as small as possible. The little girl who'd lost her mother at four years old managed to get taken in by a woman who loved her unconditionally. To disappoint her in any form was almost as devastating.

Chapter Eighteen

THE SWEET TASTE of summer had welcomed a day of unseasonably warm, sunny, blue skies that was slowly shifting to a just as comfortable evening.

Evie parked the Camaro in front of Vincent's home, in line with a train of delivery vehicles. Carlos was only seconds behind her. He brought the Chase Confections minivan to a slow-rolling stop. She assisted him with carrying the over-sized cake box, being careful moving up the bricked front steps. The entry door swung open wide before they made it to the landing. She'd received a recent picture of Vincent's sister to sculpt the cake, but it didn't do Sasha justice. The springy, scrawny little girl had grown into a tall, leggy, stunningly beautiful young woman.

"Hi, I'm—"

"I know, Vincent called me. I remember you. I didn't know you guys got back together." On a hard sigh, she flung out a hand toward the interior, beckoning them inside. "You may as well join the chaos."

They indeed entered a house of bustling activity on their way to the kitchen and set the box on the counter.

Two chefs stood at the island, working on trays of finger foods. They, along with several vendors, practically rushed

Sasha to consult on myriad party to-dos. Her frustration was apparent in her slew of curt responses.

Sasha swore fiercely under her breath. "I knew Vincent would do this. He plans a graduation party for me, then sticks me with the work. And he wouldn't let Clarice come to help. She's his housekeeper. Isn't that her job? This is what he does."

Her irritation seemed to be solely directed at her brother. Evie had received a similar call yesterday from Vincent to say he wouldn't be returning until Saturday evening. "The cake needs about another thirty minutes to fully thaw. I hope you like it."

Sasha turned to the three-foot-tall box that held her likeness within, eyes stretching, a smile following as if only just now seeing it. "I've been looking forward to this for so long."

With Carlos's help, Evie unveiled the dessert and witnessed Sasha's eyes slide even wider. "What do you think?"

"Oh snap!" Sasha palmed her mouth. "It's perfect—the cap and gown, the plaque with the tiny words listing my biomedical engineering degree, and even my braids are on point! Thank you so much." She checked her watch. "Geez, it's almost six o'clock. There's still so much to do, and I haven't even showered. The invitations said seven. People are going to start arriving. Look at this place. I'm nowhere near ready."

Vendors moved about, trying to get the place party ready. Vincent had spared no expense. Over in the living room, beyond the double set of open French doors, the landscaping and swimming pool were getting professionally decked out with a host of festive decor. A man stood at the bricked-in grill, gearing it up nice and hot. Additional cushiony lawn furniture was being carried in from one of the trucks parked out front.

Anxiousness bloomed in Sasha's eyes as two more vendors started to approach. Evie intercepted them. "Just a minute." She turned back to Sasha. "I can stick around and help if you like."

"I can't ask you to do that."

The pleading look the poor girl conveyed spoke to the contrary. Evie smiled. "You didn't ask. I offered."

"You're sure?"

"I got this. You go get yourself ready."

"Thank you." She dashed up the kitchen's spiral staircase.

Evie sent Carlos on his way then turned to the crew, who were now staring back at her. She took a breath. "Okay, who's first?" In no time she had the place in order.

Music pumped out of the indoor and outdoor speakers. A good number of guests had arrived, several dressed appropriately for the pool who dove right in. Servers circled with both virgin and spiked sangria and a host of other beverages. Evie hung back, keeping out of the way, and watched everyone having a good time from her perch on the kitchen barstool.

She looked up toward the stairs as Sasha made her entrance. Her braids were pulled up into a stylish top bun beneath a colorful hair band. The two-piece bikini with a sheer white cover-up showed off her enviously perfect, narrow figure, and held the attention of several young men.

"You look great. There are two security guards here

checking IDs and putting wrist bands on everyone. They're not messing around." Evie chuckled. "I see your brother thought of everything."

Sasha frowned. "Yeah, he's so extra. What does he think we do in college?"

"I didn't hear that." Evie laughed again. "The pitfalls of graduating at twenty."

"Anyway, Evie, thank you for helping me out. I don't know what I would've done had you not been here." She leaned her slender frame against the counter with arms folded beneath her barely B-cups. "You know, it bummed me out when you and Vin broke up back in the day. I'll bet money that it was his fault."

Evie smiled a bit awkwardly. "Breakups typically take two." A small pause shifted between them as another horde of guests filed in, many screeching excitedly at the sight of the cake on display. She stepped out of the way as Sasha got squeezed by a multitude of hugs. "Well, I'm going to head home."

"No, stay." Sasha pushed past her friends and caught Evie's hand. "Don't leave."

"I'm not dressed for it." With her hair in a ponytail loosely banded at the nape, Evie looked down at her pale pink Chase Confections T-shirt, jeans, and tan canvas sneakers. Not to mention, she was surely the oldest one here.

"Please stay. You look fine."

"From where I'm standing, she sure does."

They turned around. The sight of Vincent struck Evie like a wonderfully unexpected gift. It had been only five days, yet it felt far longer.

"I see you decided to show up," Sasha pouted, but without missing a beat, she trotted over, and hugged him, but not before delivering a light slap at his shoulder. "If it weren't for your girlfriend helping me out, my party would've been a hot mess." She hugged him again, then got pulled into the party fray outside by the pool.

"How was yo—?" Evie started, but in a flash, Vincent tugged her by the hand down a short hallway off the kitchen and into a cool, dark space. The light flickered on, revealing a well-stocked pantry. His mouth came down on hers. So hungry for his kiss, she held his face between her palms and returned the urgency, the yearning, the eager need that had only intensified with each passing day he'd been away. When she was sure the blaze would overtake her, he worked loose the button on her jeans, yanked down the zipper, and wrenched the snug fabric off her hips, taking her panties with it. With lightning speed, his slacks and boxers were at his ankles. Before she could argue that it was a bad idea, his penis was inside her, and she was taking his passion-induced, rough fucking against the door as his lips devoured hers. Their synced orgasms came quick and hard, panting, kissing, sucking in the other's oxygen. With his forehead touching hers, both needed the other to stay upright as their temperatures gradually cooled.

She reared back and gazed up at him, admiring the chiseled angles of his handsome face. "Miss me?" They laughed quietly.

"More than you know." His lips slanted over hers once more, brushing tenderly.

Someone pushed against the door, and startled, they pressed their partially nude bodies back in resistance.

"Hey, who's in there?" Sasha's voice called from the other side.

"It's me," Vincent answered, and Evie quickly dressed.

"I need to get more plastic cups. What are you doing?"

He brought up his underwear and slacks and eyed the shelves. Evie handed him the cups. He cracked open the door and shoved them at his sister.

"Is Evie with you?"

Vincent closed the door without answering. They could hear her chuckles fade with each tap of her flip-flops upon the tile floor.

"Thanks a lot," Evie whispered. "Obviously, she knows what we were doing in here."

He encircled an arm around her waist and jerked her against his chest. His mouth descended on her neck, tasting, returning that glorious buzz of yearning all over again. "We really should go check on the party."

He released her. "No way that's only thirty people."

"It's one party. And she's so happy." Evie opened the door and started out, but he caught her hand. "Babe, be nice."

"It's not that. There are still matters I'd like to discuss with you. Something came to light while working on settling your divorce."

She imagined sticking her fingers in her ears like a five-year-old. She had other plans for his first night back, and it had nothing to do with her pain-in-the-ass, officially ex-husband. "How about we enjoy the party, and tomorrow, we'll talk about whatever you want." Hesitation weighed in his gaze.

"Tomorrow then."

Chapter Nineteen

T HE ANNOYING SOUNDS like nails on a chalkboard, combined with the constant chatter, all of which seemed to be hitting Vincent's brain from every direction, woke him from a good sleep. The cleaning company he'd hired to handle the aftermath of Sasha's party had arrived and was in full swing. Why did he order a seven a.m. start time on a Sunday morning?

Finding the other side of the bed empty only added to his irritable mood. Waking Evie up with soft kisses that was sure to lead to hot morning sex would've made all the other disruptions irrelevant.

They still needed to talk. He'd played scenarios over and over on how she'd take the news about her parentage. Would she hate him for it? Maybe she'd thank him for bringing it all to light? He didn't want to destroy her relationship with her mother, even though her mother had been at the center of affecting his relationship with Evie. Regardless of the outcome, she needed to know, and he'd stalled long enough.

He got up, took a quick shower, and dressed. Midway down the stairs, he paused in surprise. The kitchen was spotless. A stroll into the living room, he found the furniture had been set back in place, floors gleamed, and the windows sparkled. Beyond the opened French doors, about a dozen workers were spread about, removing the rental items, and cleaning the grounds. In the center of it all stood Evie giving directions. She wore one of his plain white T-shirts tied into a loose side knot at her right hip and her body-hugging denims from the night before.

"She's really cool."

Vincent looked over his shoulder at Sasha in her pj's—a tank top and shorts. He frowned. "Why aren't you out there? It was your party, and it's your mess."

"I wanted to, but she said she'd see to everything, that I could go back to bed."

"Right." He side-eyed her.

"I swear." She shrugged. "Why did you guys break up before? What did you do?"

Ignoring her, Vincent stepped outside. Evie turned around from poolside. A beautiful smile highlighted her lovely features. She was amazing for sure. He took a moment to appreciate her beauty inside and out, suddenly feeling the need to capture and store it away in his memory, then went to her.

"You know you didn't have to do this."

"I don't mind."

He took her hand. "Can we talk now?" Getting a nod, he led her to his office and closed the door. His objective was firm, determined…before he stared into her beautiful eyes. Now the words seemed to get stuck behind the boulder in his throat. And underneath it was fear that she'd slip away again.

"Vincent?"

He blinked and drew on the strength that he was doing the right thing by her. "As I said, in the process of finding info on Patrick's holdings, some information came to light that I think you should know."

"I'm really not interested in anything Patrick has. Even if it's millions due me, I don't care. I want to be done with him."

"It's not that. The papers have been filed." Her brow pinched. "My guys are thorough. When I instruct them to dig into someone, they dive deep. They've never been wrong."

"Okay, what did they find? Patrick has a second family or something? Wouldn't be a great surprise." She snorted. "It might answer a few questions, frankly."

Vincent grabbed a folder from his desk and handed it to her. "It's about your adoption."

"My adoption?" She opened to a picture of the African American woman, Sonya Johnson, who, according to documents, raised Evie until the age of four years old. "How did you get a picture of my mom?"

"I believe it's an old passport photo."

She flipped through to a young photo of her *adopted* mother, Charlotte, sporting a cheerleader uniform. There were several of both young women laughing together, friends, arm in arm. She shook her head. "I don't understand. Why do you have these?"

Vincent didn't know how to say it that would not feel like a severe blow. He pointed to the picture of Charlotte. "She's your birth mother."

"No, she's not." She flapped Sonya's picture at him.

"This is my birth mother. You know that."

"Evie, my investigator discovered Charlotte gave birth to two children: you and your brother Samuel." He ushered her over to the couch, and they sat. "According to the records found, you were Charlotte Langston's firstborn."

"What? That's impossible. My mom—" She snagged the picture of Sonya holding an infant that looked to be no more than a month old. "This is my birth mother. She and my mom, er, adopted mom, were best friends since grade school. She died of leukemia. I went to live with the Langstons. You know all of this."

"Your mom…Mrs. Langston had an affair while her husband was serving overseas." Vincent fanned through the photos and documents to his claim, retrieving yet another vital piece to the puzzle. "This is a picture of your birth father. From information gathered, he and Mrs. Langston dated all throughout high school."

She tossed the folder at him and flung up from the couch, shaking her head. "That's ridiculous. Why would you even think to joke like this?"

He sat there calmly to try to help her see clearer. "I wouldn't have brought this to you if I had even the slightest doubt it wasn't true."

"Well, you've been misinformed. Whoever you have working for you obviously screwed up."

He came to his feet. "Evie, love—" he reached for her, but she jerked out of the way "—the last thing I want to do is hurt you."

"Really? From what I can see, you seem pretty damn okay with telling me about all of this, which is all nonsense.

It's no secret that you've never been a fan of my mom from day one."

"I have nothing against your mother. Though the very first day I met her, she told me in not so many words that I wasn't good enough for you."

"You stand there making false, disgusting accusations about her. Maybe I was right to listen to her back then and shouldn't change now." She flung opened the door and marched out.

Her words cut deep into an old wound, but he withstood the jagged blade and went after her. "Evie, wait." He followed her out the front entrance and jogged in his bare feet to the curb where she was digging the key to his Camaro from her pocket. "I felt you needed to know the truth."

"Yeah, right." She jumped behind the wheel and revved the engine. Her eyes met his, glistening. "Did it ever occur to you to tell your so-called infallible investigator to disregard those findings? To concentrate on doing his damn job, which was to get information on Patrick? Isn't that what he was hired to do? That you would take his word as law instead of considering my feelings is unconscionable. If this misinformation were to get back to my family…" Her voiced trembled.

"I've never half-stepped with any of my clients. My firm is successful because I go the extra mile, and I've earned that reputation in this city. I say that to say, in my role as your attorney, it is my duty to provide you that same level of service. That's what I'm doing here, looking out for your best interest."

"I see." Her lips thinned, matching the scathing look in

her eyes. "You are more concerned about being the top dog at your firm. Vincent Scott, Mr. High and Mighty, attorney at law. Are you proud of yourself?"

"I did consider how this would affect you. But—" He had to leap out of the way when she floored it. *Fuck.* He went back inside. Sasha stood in the entryway, sipping a cup of coffee.

"Evie seems in a hurry. Everything okay?"

"Peachy," he muttered on his way to his office and slammed the door.

EVIE ENTERED HER home, her mind still whirling with flashes of the photos she'd seen. She paced her kitchen tile. It simply couldn't be true. The woman who'd sheltered and helped push away the grave panic and pain of that little girl's loss as her tiny world crumbled down around her would never be so cruel. Yet she found herself pulling up her mom's number on her cell phone.

"Hi, honey. I can't talk right now. I'm late for my yoga class." Her voiced sounded a bit winded around the double chirp of her car's keyless remote.

"This won't take long. Who's my mother?"

She chuckled. "What kind of silly question is that?"

"Who gave birth to me?"

"Evie, where is this coming from?"

"Does Dad know you cheated on him, that I'm the result of your infidelity?" Her ticking silence practically screamed the answer. "Well?"

"Who told you this?"

Her body shook as her anguished heart plummeted into her stomach. "You want to know who told me? Vincent Scott. And you know what else? He's an attorney now. He's also a damn good mechanic. But I couldn't see that because of you. Now answer the damn question! I want to hear you say it! I need you to say it!" she yelled, hot tears burning down her cheeks.

"I-I did. I gave birth to you."

Shattered, wailing, doubling over, Evie felt she was going to be sick. "Then...then, my mom...Sonya was just some woman—" her cries broke between each word "—some woman for you to dump me on?"

"Sonya was my best friend since grade school. She was like my sister. I was devastated when she died."

"Yeah, because you could no longer hide me, hide your mistake." Her head swam, and her stomach roiled like she'd just ingested a toxic meal.

"You were never a mistake. I didn't want an abortion. But I got scared and didn't know how to fix it. Sonya and I decided she'd raise you. We weren't thinking smart...I wasn't thinking smart. I was selfish. I wanted to finish school."

Evie took a deep breath to try to calm her shivers of grief, but it didn't halt the tears. "You're right, you were only thinking about yourself. Does Dad know? What about Sam? And Grandma? The rest of the family? Am I the only one in the dark?"

"No one knows. As for the affair, when your father returned from his tour, I think he had his suspensions. I was spending a lot of time over at Sonya's, so I could be with you. I wanted my baby girl. It killed me when I'd have to leave without you." Her voice shook. "Your father thought I was sneaking around on him."

"You'd already done that," Evie muttered, slapping away more tears.

"The family are all in Arizona. I lived in New York, but I stayed with Sonya in South Carolina during my pregnancy. Sonya moved to New York after you were born. That way I could see you."

"And Dad doesn't know any of this?"

"No, he doesn't know you're my biological daughter. Sweetheart, I was so young. I chose to marry safe instead of for love. Don't misunderstand me. Things got better between your father and me. I love him, and he's been a good husband and father to you and Samuel. But in the beginning, that wasn't the case for me. I loved someone else. His name was Julius Mitchell. He was African American. We dated on and off throughout high school. He—"

"Stop!" Evie screamed. A cold sweat broke out over her skin; the room spun. She jabbed the phone, putting it on speaker, and bent over, clutching her knees.

"What I did, letting you think you were adopted, it's selfish and unforgivable, I know." She cried. "But I'm hoping you can find a way to forgive me. You mean the world to me."

"You're right." Evie swallowed hard repeatedly to halt the bile rising in her throat. "What you did was selfish and unforgivable. I don't have a mother." She disconnected. Her trembling legs gave out, sliding her down the cabinet to the floor where she sat. Her forehead pressed atop bent knees, her arms shrouding her ears to try to block out her loud wails.

Chapter Twenty

VINCENT STRODE AROUND his pool, watching the soft ripples in the water. Lights within the landscaping flickered on. Dusk had fallen into darkness, erasing shadows. He couldn't eat, couldn't sleep. To simply hear her voice would be enough to kickstart his will to breathe easy.

With his phone to his ear, he held on to hope that this time Evie would pick up. Several rings said hope apparently wasn't on his side. Once again, it went to voicemail. To leave another message to add to the twenty or so previous ones he'd left that had gone unanswered would be pointless. Yet, he did so anyway, then went inside.

"Any luck?" Trenton asked, seated on the couch.

Vincent shook his head and slouched in the chair.

Dominic returned from the bathroom and dropped down next to his brother. "Did you talk—?" Trenton gave him an elbow nudge.

Through their wives, they'd learned Evie had cut things off with him. The guys had come over to watch the game and to offer support, but all Vincent wanted was to be left alone. Since they weren't going to leave until he talked it out, he went with it. "She feels I should have told Will to back off, leave the info about her parentage alone. I believe she would've preferred to stay in the dark about it all. Was I not supposed to do my job effectively? Half-ass her case? She wanted a damn good attorney. It's what she got."

"You were being upfront with her," Trenton said. "She can't fault you for that."

Dominic sat forward. "Vin, man, sorry, bro. To find out that your mom gave you to her best friend to hide an affair, then pretended you were adopted after the friend died to continue hiding her wrongdoings, no doubt, that's some heavy shit to get over."

"Give her time. As Dom said, she's dealing with a lot," Trenton assured him.

The agonizing pressure weighing on Vincent's chest had become damn near unbearable. He could barely catch his breath.

I've lost her again.

LIGHT STRUCK BEHIND Evie's eyelids from the sudden flick of the lamp. She brought the covers up to her neck and buried her face into the pillow, curling into her dark corner. Not sure when day had turned to night.

"You didn't eat your dinner." Kennedi regarded the tray she'd set on the table by the window over an hour ago. Cold grilled chicken and mixed vegetables sat untouched.

"I'm not hungry," Evie murmured, her throat raw from the continuous flow of tears.

Tabitha came forward and picked up the litter of crumpled, discarded tissues from the floor and tossed the wad into the wastebasket, then eased down on the edge of the bed. A soothing hand tenderly caressed Evie's shoulder. "I won't even pretend to know the pain you're going through." Her voice was the softest it'd ever been. "By the way, your brother called me. He's been trying to reach you. He wants you to give him a ring."

"We wish there was more we could do." Kennedi sat at her feet. "Just know we're here for you. Whatever you need."

Evie's cell phone on the nightstand rang.

Tabitha checked the display. "It's Vincent again. Let me answer it just to check in with him for you."

"Don't." Evie rolled over and met her friends' concerned gazes. "I can't figure out why he did it. What did he have to gain?" She swallowed hard. The ache surrounding her heart had gotten so tight it was hard to exhale around it. "Stopping Patrick should've been his focus, not tearing apart my family."

"Trent always says Vincent's thorough." Kennedi shrugged lightly, awkwardly. "A stickler. He leaves no stone unturned."

"Yes, I see that, regardless who he hurts in the process," Evie gritted. "We were happy. We were rebuilding our life together. My feelings, our relationship—it all meant so little to him. When he spoke about his firm, its reputation, it seemed more important to maintain an image than anything. His callousness toward me… He once said the law profession robs one of one's soul. He's become that man."

"That's a bit harsh, don't you think?" Tabitha questioned, never holding anything back. "Maybe you should sit down and have a conversation with him about it all."

Evie reached to the nightstand for her phone. "I need to call my brother."

"And Vincent?" Kennedi asked.

She stared back at them as the line connected.

"Hi, Sam."

THE NEXT MORNING Evie awoke bathed in sweat from the terror of her reoccurring nightmare. But it was a harsh memory—that terrified little girl unable to shake her mom from a dead sleep on the couch. Her endless screams and panicky breaths at seeing the emergency responder drape the white sheet over her mom's head. But Sonya wasn't her mom. That little girl was all alone. Then Charlotte's face appeared, saving her from the darkness.

Heart heavy, it hurt to move. But she forced herself up and got into the shower. With eyes closed, she took a moment to soak up the relaxing warmth that licked her skin, then used the razor to remove the leg stubble before running the loofah over her body.

After a quick shampoo and conditioner, restoring her thick mane to soft, bouncy curls, she split the strands down the center and worked the locks into two side braids, then dressed in a plain T-shirt and knit shorts. When she was done, the suffocating veil of sadness lifted just enough to allow her to breathe a bit easier.

She went back in the bedroom. Kennedi was there smoothing freshly changed bedding and fluffing the pillows against the headboard.

"I'm going to get you something to eat after I start these to wash." She scooped the sheets from the floor.

"No. I'll come down." She was determined to maintain the consistent, even breaths that managed to roll from her chest without breaking.

Tabitha entered. "Evie, there's someone here to see you."

Evie tensed and shrunk back. "I don't want—" Her eyes watered instantly at the sight of the figure that appeared in the doorway. "Dad?"

"Hi, buttercup." He came forward and pulled her into his protective embrace, and they clung tight to one another. The door clank against the latch. They looked up to see they were alone. Warm blue eyes regarded her. "Your mother told me everything. I tried calling you."

A flood of tears fell. "I thought if you found out, you wouldn't want to be my dad anymore."

"That's utterly absurd, and it's why I came." He grabbed a tissue from the box on the nightstand and dried her cheeks, then guided her to sit on the bench at the foot of the bed. "Listen, you're my daughter, my buttercup. Nothing will ever change that." His tone was firm, yet his eyes gleamed.

"What Mom did to you…what she did to both of us…"

"Yes, what she did was awful. But she was young when we got married. I went off on my first tour a month into it. Back then, making rank was most important. My military career took priority. Then you came into my life, and everything changed. Having you made me realize what was really important."

"You forgive her?"

"It's going to take time to mend the cracks, but I will. I

know she misses the daily chats you two used to have. And watching TV shows together."

"I miss her, too, but I don't know if I can get past what she did. She gave me away." Evie sucked back more tears.

He took her hand, stroking his thumb across her knuckles. "I know you're hurting. So am I. One thing I know for certain is she loves us. Your mother wanted to come down today, but I felt I should see you first, discuss this with you. I also wanted to talk to you about the young man you're seeing, or should I say seeing again." He cut a light smile. "I'm told he was the one who brought all of this to the forefront. He's an attorney now, I hear."

"Yes." Her throat tightened. "I'm not... We're not together."

His head angled, then he nodded. "He did the right thing. If you'd found out he knew about this and didn't share it with you, what would you have done? Trust, sweetheart. That's what he showed here. It must have been difficult for him knowing the pain it would cause you. Loyal. Protective. That's the sort of man I want for you. From where I sit, he's demonstrated that."

"I thought you didn't like Vincent."

He drew back. "I never said that. If I recall, I said I found him to be a bit too serious, that he could loosen up. But a decent fellow. No man will ever check all the boxes, be good enough for my buttercup." He winked.

"It was Mom." Evie frowned, still holding on to hurt and discontent. "She ruined things with Vincent and me back then and has done so again now."

He laid his hand atop their linked ones. "She only wants

what's best for you. It's going to take time for you to rebuild what has broken between you two. Just promise me you'll work on it."

If her dad could forgive so freely, she could try. "I guess."

Chapter Twenty-One

THE DOORBELL RANG.

Vincent lay stretched out on the couch, staring at the TV, not really watching. Low, gray clouds turned the late afternoon into a dreary landscape, matching his mood.

The chime came again just as the first fat droplets of rain splashed in the swimming pool, then quickly began hammering the pavers. It was likely the fellas stopping by to check on him. They'd get the hint and bounce when they realized he wouldn't bother to give them shelter.

He'd delegated his workload at the office and had taken a few days off, shutting down all communication. All he wanted to do was lie still, hardly even breathe, to keep a check on his emotions. So far, he'd failed miserably. Every time he closed his eyes, he could almost feel the gentleness of Evie's touch, hear the tenderness in her voice. To have found her and lost her again was beyond devastating. And of his own doing.

The tap on the French door jolted him upright. Evie stood on the other side of the glass, hair whipping in the wind and rain. Vincent leaped across the room and pulled it open.

"Thanks." She shivered with shy glances up at him. "I

know I shouldn't have invaded your home."

"Let me get you a towel." He jetted upstairs. As his shock at seeing her started to settle, he grabbed one of his sister's T-shirts and shorts, then snagged a couple of bath towels. He returned and gestured around his home. "You know where the bathrooms are. Please, help yourself. Can I get you something to drink?"

"No, thanks. Is anyone here? Sasha?"

"She's with her friends in New Orleans. I gave my housekeeper time off. It's just me." He watched as she removed her glasses, toed off her soaked canvas sneakers, and stripped out of her clothes down to her bra and panties, then quickly dressed. Within seconds, she'd braided and tucked her hair into a twisted knot at the nape. "I'll throw these in the dryer." He scooped up the wet garments and jogged off. When he returned, she was sitting on edge of the couch with hands tightly linked, atop the blanket that had been his bed for the past two days. He eased down beside her and said softly, "The last thing I wanted to do was hurt you."

"I know. Well, I realize that now."

"Have you spoken to your mother?"

"Not since I confronted her about everything. It's a big part of what hurts—she and I are in this weird place. I don't want to talk to her, but I feel empty not talking to her. We used to speak or text every single day. We watched movies together over video chat." She glanced up from her linked hands with a soft smile. "She has a thing for Shemar Moore. Our closeness is gone now." Her voice trembled.

He caressed a tentative hand across her slumped shoulders. "You'll get back what you had with her. It'll just take time."

She met his gaze, glittering green irises swimming in tears. "When you told me about my parentage—"

"Evie, I—" She pressed a light finger across his lips.

"Please, I need to say this. I got so frightened. I was sure I'd lose my family, my dad, everything I cherish. It also brought forward the fight you and I had those many years ago. I tried to get you to return to college, fit into my family's mold, because I feared if you didn't, I'd have to choose between you and them. I realize now that simply wasn't the case. I was always impressed by the work you did at the garage. It was never about that.

"What I'm trying to say is, I'm sorry for the hurtful things I said then and those I said recently."

When she quieted, Vincent took her hand. "I was so narrowly focused on following my rulebook, my war sheet, that I didn't even consider shutting down the investigation, order my guy to detour from your family and stick only to finding info on Patrick. It's what I should've done. I'm sorry, and I'll make you this promise. Never again will I let my work come before your feelings. I love you, Evie. It's always been you."

"I love you, too, Vincent."

He didn't have to ask for her touch or her kiss. She offered it fully, to the edge of breathlessness. Their hands moved slowly over one another, undressing, tugging until they were both naked. Their bodies joined, twining tightly together, as they took advantage of every limited inch of width of the cushions.

Vincent wanted to take his time, savor having her beneath him, relish the sensation of being buried deep inside her once again, and marvel at the feel of her delicate strokes upon his body, but the swirl of his emotions was hurling everything off-balance. He'd missed her so damn much, every nerve seemed amplified as his hips pumped within the soft curves of her thighs with a swift, jerky rhythm.

"Vinny," she whispered, her arms skating over the slick sheen of his shoulders. Her legs wrapped around his back. Her body arched with each undulation, hands cupping his rear, meeting his severe thrusts again and again. Together, through ragged pants, their climax splintered into a prism of pleasurable pieces.

His muscle went slack beneath his fevered skin as he felt himself slipping free from the warmth of her body.

She nuzzled the side of his neck, the touch of her lips maddeningly soft. "I missed you like crazy."

"That makes two of us." He smoothed the stray damp hairs from her brow and shifted on his side, taking her with him, not wishing to let go, and feeling immensely content. "I took some time away from the office because I couldn't focus. You're all I could think about. I thought I'd lost you again."

"Never."

"Marry me, Evie."

She blinked. And blinked again. "Vincent." Her lips met his, their mouths mating tenderly.

He opened for her tongue, sucking her in, drugging himself with the sweet taste of her then broke away after deliciously long minutes. Her eyes fluttered open, and he asked, smiling, "Is that a yes?"

"A thousand times, yes."

Chapter Twenty-Two

E VIE GLANCED AT the bedside clock.

"It's almost noon. We probably should at least make an attempt to do something productive today. We haven't left your bed in two days." Straddling his hips, she gave the moist heat of his neck a gentle nibble, while letting their sweaty satiated bodies cool by the aid of comforting AC.

"Madam, I beg to differ. We've been very productive." Vincent's strong arms wrapped around her, the fine hairs on his chest teasing her overly sensitive nipples that he'd been fondling and sucking to deliciously stiff peaks. "We've made love, which is a major workout." He grinned and trailed warm fingertips on both hands down her spine, drew teasingly slow circles over her bare buttocks, then trekked his tender touches back up. "We've ordered in, showered together, watched a little TV, and made love some more. I say we've been quite productive."

Their cell phones on the nightstand seemed to ring sim-ultaneously.

Evie reached for hers that flashed Tabitha's name, but Vincent caught her hand. "Don't answer it," he said, noting Trenton's name pop up on his. "We'll check in with them later." His hand slid between their bodies and guided his penis inside her where he'd already stroked her passion raw.

She rocked slowly, but then lifted off him before the sensations could overtake her. "It's been days. We should let them know we're fine." She grabbed her phone and called Tabitha. It connected within short rings. "Hey, Tab. I'm at Vincent's." She jumped at the pinch to her butt, and looked back at Vincent's smiling face, stretched out with his arms crossed above his head. "Behave," she whispered.

"Kennedi's father passed away."

"Oh no!" Evie turned to Vincent. "Kennedi's father passed." He leaped up and grabbed his cell phone.

"How's Kennedi?" she asked while observing Vincent across the room talking to Trenton.

"As good as can be expected. Dom and I are headed over to her now."

"I'm on my way." Evie went to Vincent, who just ended his call as well. "I have to get home to change before I go to her."

"Of course."

Chapter Twenty-Three

Vincent came downstairs. Evie lay stretched out on his couch beneath the throw, the afternoon sun beaming in on her lovely face as she watched one of her crime dramas. Her mood hadn't improved much following the funeral a few weeks ago.

Their relationship was good, better than good. But losing a parent, even if it wasn't to death, weighed on her. As close as she'd been with her mother, the grief she was suffering was real.

How she'd take what he was about to tell her was a fifty-fifty toss-up. One thing was certain, by his calculation, he had less than fifteen minutes to come clean.

He took the remote and put the show on pause.

She sat up. "Babe, I'm watching that."

"I know. I'm sorry. There's something I need to tell you." Panic registered in her stare. He'd said those very words once before, and it didn't end well. He sat and took her hands in his. "I know you've been down about everything that happened between you and your mother. When Kennedi's father passed, you were upset for her, but I could see it also affected you. You miss your mother."

"I do, but I don't know where to start."

"How about at the beginning?"

The doorbell rang. *She's early.*

Evie glanced in the direction of the entryway. "Who's that?"

Vincent stood up. "I'll be right back." He jogged to the door, then returned. "That's what I wanted to tell you. I invited your mother to come visit." He stepped aside, revealing Mrs. Langston.

"Hello, sweetheart." Her mother's cautious gaze lingered on her daughter.

Vincent held his breath through ticking silence as Evie just stood there. Had he made the wrong call? Then she slowly came forward and encircled her arms around his neck, tucking her face beneath his chin. "Thank you. I love you so much," she murmured.

He charted the smooth curve of her cheek with his thumb. "I love you, too, and would do anything just to see you smile."

She pressed a kiss to his lips before moving to her mother. As Vincent observed the two embracing, he let go a quiet breath.

He had Evie, the woman who lit and warmed his soul. The promise of their future was strong.

Epilogue

"EVIE, DAD SAID the burgers are ready," Sam called from the threshold of the open French doors.

"We're almost done." Evie pulled the baked beans from the oven. "Think we have enough sides?" she asked her mom and Kennedi, as well as Mrs. Scott, her future mother-in-law who was putting the finishing garnish on her scrumptious lump crabmeat casserole.

"There's plenty," Charlotte said while topping off the frosting on the carrot cake.

"More than enough. I'll start getting these to the table." Mrs. Scott cradled the dish of crab deliciousness and grabbed a package of bread buns.

"I'll help you." Kennedi scooped two side dishes from among the horde on the kitchen island and followed her outside.

"Mom, taste this." Evie fed her a dollop of potato salad. "Is it as good as yours?"

"Yum, you nailed it. It's perfect."

"Really?" Evie smiled. She'd made the dish numerous times but could never get the recipe quite right. It helped to have her mom as a guide, offering, "a pinch of this and a dash of that." After all, it was a family recipe. But it was simply wonderful to have her here. Over the past four months, they'd worked hard to mend their relationship. Their connection, their bond was returning.

Her parents were reconciling their union as well through counseling. It seemed to be working.

"Need any help?"

Evie turned her head to Tabitha coming down the spiral stairs. She'd gone up to breastfeed little Dominic and put him down for a nap, not that the six-week-old did much else. Evie's godson had arrived a couple weeks early but was a welcome addition, nonetheless. "Good timing. We're ready to eat."

They brought the remaining side dishes outside to the long table.

Vincent came up behind her and circled his arms around her waist, delivering a kiss on her cheek. "Our dads have been comparing grilling techniques." They looked on as the two men laughingly debated. Vincent chuckled, amplifying the smile that seemed to be forever imprinted in his features. "They each swear we'll be able to taste the difference."

Smiling, Evie reared her head back and caught his peck on the lips. "I guess we will see."

He clasped her hand and straightened the six-carat Asscher-cut diamond solitaire on her finger, then lowered his head and whispered at her ear, "So, how do you want to do this?"

She regarded Sasha chatting with the young man she'd invited and who Vincent kept a keen eye on; Kennedi and Trenton, the pair arm in arm; Tabitha and Dominic, the happy, new parents of a beautiful baby boy; her brother,

Samuel, and his wife, Robbie, teasing one another; Vincent's parents, their strong affection easily conveyed in their shared smiles; and her parents standing side by side, holding each other's gaze, a loving look she'd witnessed growing up a thousand times over—a mingle of joyful faces.

"We'll do this like we do everything—together."

Everyone began digging in. When plates where piled high and seats were occupied, Vincent tapped the side of his wineglass with his fork, muting the chatter. He came to his feet, and Evie joined him, their hands entwined.

"Evie and I want to thank you all for being here on this beautiful afternoon. As you know, our wedding date is about a month away. We'd like to share that five months…" He looked at Evie.

She shrugged. "And a half."

"Five and a half months thereafter, we'll host another celebration to welcome our firstborn."

A resounding gasp floated around the table, then chairs screeched across the pavers and Evie was smothered in a rush of bodies, all giving her hugs and kisses. Vincent received his share of the same, a blissful swaddle of love and well-wishes.

Later that night when the house was quiet, and they'd settled in bed, cuddling together in a relaxing sprawl, Evie looked up at her loving fiancé. "That went well. Our families actually like each other."

He drew back. "You thought they wouldn't?"

"My dad can sometimes be very regimented, but I see your dad held his own."

"I had no doubt. Which burger was better? My dad's or yours?"

She grinned. "I didn't taste a difference."

"Same."

They laughed.

Vincent reached to the lamp and clicked off the light then drew her back into his strong arms.

Moonlight lifted the darkness, filtering in through the window, casting the room in a soft, romantic glimmer.

"I love you, Evie."

"I love you, too."

"I promise to make you happy until my last breath."

"You more than make me happy."

Happy was too weak a word to describe the immense joy Evie felt. It was as though every pore was saturated, filling her up to near bursting with light. Each one of the people who had gathered around them today were contributors to the glow permeating outward. But it was the man lying beside her that created the warmth in her soul, completed every breath she took, kept the fire burning in her eyes, and drenched her heart with love. Instead of that one simple word, she let those intense feelings be her definition.

The End

Want more? Check out Dominic and Tabitha's story in *Catch Me*!

Join Tule Publishing's newsletter for more great reads and weekly deals!

If you enjoyed *Return to Me,*
you'll love the other books in....

The Tycoon's Temptation series

Book 1: *See Me*

Book 2: *Catch Me*

Book 3: *Return to Me*

Available now at your favorite online retailer!

About the Author

Award winning author, Michele Arris, has always had a
fondness for romance and happy endings.

"I love to write stories where my characters are guaranteed
their happily ever after."

When Michele isn't seated in front of her computer, shaping
bad-ass alpha heroes who meet their match in strong,
hardworking heroines, she enjoys reading all types of
romance genres, watching period classics, actually looks
forward to working out, which is where she spends time
coming up with a lot of her story ideas, is a vitamin junkie,
and loves spending time with family and friends – simply
enjoying life.

Michele lives in the Washington D.C. area. Get to know
more about her by visiting her website at michelearris.com.

Thank you for reading

Return to Me

If you enjoyed this book, you can find more from all our great authors at TulePublishing.com, or from your favorite online retailer.

Made in the USA
Columbia, SC
13 July 2022

63430620R00140